The Key to My Heart

"In our town, if you cough in the High Street the chemist up at the Town Hall has got a bottle of cough mixture wrapped up and waiting for you." And nobody in the town provides such a wealth of delicious gossip as "Noisy" Brackett and his wife Sally. Refusing to pay her bills, chasing her errant husband round the countryside in fast cars, setting fire to the heart of Bob, the local baker, Sally is a gloriously raffish figure of fun. In this comedy in three parts Bob relates how Sally finally paid his account, how Noisy got off a motoring charge by sneezing, stole a case of stuffed birds from his own house, and barricaded himself in a cottage with a cardboard Argentinian air-hostess to foil Sally's pursuit.

THE KEY
TO MY HEART

A Comedy in Three Parts

V. S. PRITCHETT

Illustrated by
PAUL HOGARTH

1963
CHATTO & WINDUS
LONDON

Published by
Chatto and Windus Ltd
42 William IV Street
London WC2

*

Clarke, Irwin & Co Ltd
Toronto

CONTENTS

To My Wife

The author makes acknowledgments to the Editors of *The New Yorker* and *Argosy* in which these stories originally appeared

THE KEY TO MY HEART

1

The Key to My Heart

WHEN Father dropped dead and Mother and I
were left to run the business on our own, I was
twenty-four years old. It was the principal bakery in our
town, a good little business, and Father had built it up
from nothing. Father used to wink at me when Mother
talked about their "first wedding". "How many times
have you been married? Who was it that time?" he
used to say to her. She was speaking of the time they
first ventured out of the bakery into catering for weddings and local dances. For a long time, when I was a
child, we lived over the shop; then Mother made Father
take a house down the street. Later still, we opened a
café next door but two to the shop, and our idea was to
buy up the two little places in between. But something
went wrong in the last years of Father's life. Working
at night in the heat and getting up at the wrong time of
day disorganized him. And then the weddings were his
downfall. There is always champagne left over at weddings, and Father got to like it and live on it. And then
brandy followed. When Mr. Pickering, the solicitor,
went into the will and the accounts, there was muddle
everywhere, and bills we had never heard of came in.

"Father kept it all in his head," Mother said, very
proud of him for that. Mr. Pickering and I had to sort it
all out, and one of the things we discovered was that
what we owed was nothing to what people owed us.
Mother used to serve in the shop and do the books. She
did it, we used to say, for the sake of the gossip—to

11

daydream about why the schoolmistress ordered crumpets only on Thursdays, or guessing, if someone ordered more of this kind of cake or that, who was going to eat it with them. She was generally right, and she knew more about what was going on in the town than anyone else. As long as the daily and weekly customers paid their books, she didn't bother; she hated sending bills, and she was more pleased than upset when Mr. Pickering told her there was a good six hundred pounds owing by people who either hadn't been asked to pay or who were simply not troubling themselves. In a small business, this was a lot of money. It was the rich and the big pots in the country who were the worst of these debtors. Dad and Mother never minded being owed by the rich. They had both grown up in the days when you were afraid of offending people, and to hear my mother talk you would have thought that by asking the well-off to fork out you were going to kill the goose that lays the golden egg, knock the bottom out of society, and let a Labour government in.

"Think of what they have to pay in taxes," she would say, pitying them. "And the death duties!" And when I did what Mr. Pickering said, and sent out accounts to these people, saying politely that it had no doubt been overlooked, Mother looked mournful and said getting a commission in the Army had turned my head. The money came in, of course. When Colonel Williams paid up and didn't dispute it, Mother looked at his cheque as if it were an insult from the old gentleman and, in fact, "lost" it in her apron pocket for a week. Lady Littlebank complained, but she paid all the same. A few did not answer, but when I called at their houses they paid at once. Though the look on Mother's face was as much as to say I was a son ruining her lifework and destroying

her chances of holding her head up in society. At the end
of two or three months there was only one large account
outstanding—a Mrs. Brackett's. Mrs. Brackett did not
answer, and you can guess Mother made the most of
this. Mother spoke highly of Mrs. Brackett, said she was
"such a lady", "came of a wonderful family", and once
even praised her clothes. She was the richest woman in
the county, and young. She became my mother's ideal.

Mrs. Brackett was married to a pilot and racing
motorist known in the town as Noisy Brackett; it was
she, as my mother said, nodding her head up and down,
who "had the money". Noisy was given a couple of cars
and his pocket money, but, having done that, Mrs.
Brackett paid as little as she could, as slowly as she
could, to everyone else. When I talked about her
account to other shopkeepers in the town, they put on
their glasses, had a look at their books, sniffed, and said
nothing. Every shopkeeper, my father used to say,
woke up in the early hours of the morning thinking of
how much she owed him, and dreaming of her fortune.
You can work out how long her bill with us had run on
when I say it was nearly two hundred and thirty pounds.
The exact sum was two hundred and twenty-eight pounds
fourteen and fourpence. I shall always remember it.

The first time I made out Mrs. Brackett's bill, I gave
it to Noisy. He often came into the café to flirt with the
girls, or to our shop to see Mother and get her to cash
cheques for him. He was a thin little man, straight as a
stick and looked as brittle, and covered (they said) with
scars and wounds from his crashes. He had the curly
shining black hair of a sick gypsy, and the lines of a
charmer all over his face. His smiles quickly ended in a
sudden, stern twitching of his left cheek and eye, like the
crack of a whip, which delighted the women. He was a

dandy, and from Mother he had the highest praise she could give to any man. He was, she said, "snobby".

When I gave Noisy our bill, he handed it back to me at once. "Be a sweetie-pie," he said, "and keep it under your hat until the day after tomorrow. Tomorrow's my payday, and I don't want the Fairy Queen to get her mind taken off it—d'you follow? Good! Fine! Splendid fellow! Bang on!" And, with a twitch, he was back in his long white Bentley. "Bring it yourself," he said, looking me up and down. I am a very tall man, and little Noisy had a long way to look. "It'll do the trick."

Noisy did not hide his dependence on his wife. Every-one except the local gentry liked him.

So on the Thursday, when the shop was closed and I could leave the café to the waitresses—a good pair of girls, and Rosie, the dark one, very pretty—I took the station wagon and drove up to Heading Mount, four miles out of the town. It was June; they were getting the hay in. The land in the valley fetches its price—you wouldn't believe it if I told you what a farm fetches there. Higher up, the land is poor, where the oak woods begin, and all that stretch that belonged to old Mr. Lucas, Mrs. Brackett's father, who had made a fortune out of machine tools. The estate was broken up when he died. I came out of the oak woods and turned into the drive, which winds between low stone walls and tall rhododendron bushes, so that it is like a damp, dark sunken lane, and very narrow. Couples often walked up on Sundays in June to see the show of rhododendrons on the slopes at Heading; the bushes were in flower as I drove by. I was speeding to the sharp turn at the end of the drive, before you come to the house, when I had to brake suddenly. Mrs. Brackett's grey Bentley was drawn broadside across it, blocking the drive completely. I ought to have seen this was a bad omen.

To leave a car like that, anywhere, was typical of Mrs. Brackett. If there was a traffic jam in the town, or if someone couldn't get into the market, nine times out of ten Mrs. Brackett's car was the cause. She just stepped out of it wherever it was, as if she were dropping her coat off for someone else to pick up. The police did nothing. As she got back in, she would smile at them, raise one eyebrow, wag her hips, and let them see as much of her legs as she thought fit for the hour of the day, and drive off with a small wave of her hand that made them swell with apologies and blow up someone else. Sometimes she went green with a rage that was terrifying coming from so small a person.

As I walked across the lawn, I realized I had missed the back lane to the house, and that I ought to have driven along a wire-fenced road across the fields to the farm and the kitchen, where the housekeeper lived. But I had not been up there for several years, and had forgotten it. As I walked toward the white front door, I kicked a woman's shoe—a shoe for a very small foot. I picked it up. I was a few yards from the door when Mrs. Brackett marched out, stopped on the steps, and then, as sharp as a sergeant, shouted, "Jimmy!" She was looking up at the sky, as though she expected to bring her husband down out of it.

She was barefooted, wearing a blue-and-white checked shirt and dusty jeans, and her short fair hair untidy, and she was making an ugly mouth, like a boy's, on her pretty face. I was holding out the shoe as I went forward. There was no answer to her shout. Then she saw me and stared at the shoe.

"Who are you? What are you doing with that?" she asked. "Put it down."

15

But before I could answer, from the other side of the buildings there was the sound of a car starting and driving off on the back road. Mrs. Brackett heard this. She turned and marched into the house again, but in a few seconds she returned, running past me across the lawn. She jumped into her car, backed—and then she saw mine blocking the drive. She sounded her horn, again and again. A dog barked, and she jumped out and bawled at me. "You bloody fool!" she shouted. "Get that van of yours out of the way!"

The language that came out of her small mouth was like what you hear in the cattle market on Fridays. I slowly went up and got into my van. I could hear her swearing and the other car tearing off; already it must have turned into the main road. I got into mine, and there we sat, face to face, scowling at each other through our windscreens. I reversed down the long, winding drive, very fast, keeping one eye on her all the time, and turned sharply off the road at the entrance. I don't mind saying I was showing off. I can reverse a car at speed and put it anywhere to within an inch of where I want to. I saw her face change as she came on, for in her temper she was coming fast down the drive straight at me, radiator to radiator. At the end, she gave one glance of surprise at me, and I think held back a word she had ready as she drove past. At any rate, her mouth was open. Half a dozen cows started from under the trees and went trotting round the field in panic as she went, and the rooks came out of the elms like bits of black paper.

By bad luck, you see, I had arrived in the middle of one of the regular Brackett rows. They were famous in the neighbourhood. The Bracketts chased each other round the house, things came out of windows—clothes,

boots, anything. Our roundsman said he had once seen a portable radio, playing full on, come flying out, and that it had fallen, still playing, in the roses. Servants came down to the town and said they had had enough of it. Money was usually at the bottom of the trouble. There was a tale going round that when a village girl who worked there got married, Mrs. Brackett gave her a three-shilling alarm clock for a wedding present.

The rows always went the same way. A car would race out of the drive with Noisy in it, and five minutes later Mrs. Brackett would be in her car chasing him, and no one was safe on the roads for twenty miles around. Sometimes it might end quietly in a country pub, with Mrs. Brackett in one bar and Noisy in the other, white-faced and playing hymns on the piano to mock her until she gave in. Other times, it might go on through the night. Noisy, who raced cars, was the better driver, but she was wilder. She would do anything—she once cut through the footpath of the cemetery to catch him on the other side. She sometimes caught him, but more than once her meanness about money would leave her standing. There would be a telephone call to Briggs's garage: Mrs. Brackett had run out of petrol. She was too mean ever to have much more than a gallon in the tank.

"Bless her," Noisy used to say if anyone mentioned these chases to him. "I always rely on the Fairy Queen to run out of gas."

Noisy was a woman-hater. His trouble was his habit of saying "Bless you" to the whole female sex.

"Well, I hope you're satisfied," my mother said when I got home. I put Mrs. Brackett's shoe on the table.

"I've made some progress," I said.

My mother looked at the shoe for a long time. Now that I had got something out of Mrs. Brackett, Mother began to think a little less of her. "You'd think a woman with feet like that would dress better," she said.

But what annoyed me was that at some stage in the afternoon's chase Noisy had slipped in and got Mother to cash him a cheque for twenty pounds.

June is the busy time of the year for us. There are all the June weddings. Noisy and Mrs. Brackett must have settled down again somehow, because I saw them driving through the town once or twice. I said to myself, "You wait till the rush is over."

In July, I went up to the Bracketts' house a second time. Rosie, the dark girl who works in our café, came with me, because she wanted to meet her aunt at the main-line station, three or four miles over the hill beyond Heading Mount, and I was taking her on there after I had spoken to Mrs. Brackett. I drove up to the house. The rhododendrons had died, and there were pods on them already going brown. The sun struck warm in front of the house. It was wonderfully quiet.

I left the girl in the car, reading a book, and was working out a sentence to say, when I saw Mrs. Brackett kneeling by a goldfish pond, at the far side of the great lawn. She turned and saw me. I did not know whether to go over the lawn to her or to wait where I was. I decided to go over, and she got up and walked to me. Mother was right about her clothes. This time she was wearing a gaudy tomato-coloured cotton dress that looked like someone else's, and nothing on underneath it. I do not know why it was—whether it was because I was standing on the grass as she was walking over, whether it was my anxiety about how to begin the conversation, or whether it was because of her bare white arms, the dawdling manner of her walk, and the inquisitiveness of her eyes—but I thought I was going to faint.

When she was two yards away, my heart jumped, my throat closed, and my head was swimming. Although I had often seen her driving through the town, and though I remembered our last meeting all too well, I had never really looked at her before. She stopped, but I had the feeling that she had not stopped, but was invisibly walking on until she walked clean through me. My arms went weak. She was amused by the effect she had on me.

"I know who you are," she said. "You are Mr. Fraser's son. Do you want to speak to me?"

I did, but I couldn't. I forgot all the sentences I had prepared. "I've come about our cheque," I said at last. I shouted it. Mrs. Brackett was as startled by my shout as I was. She blushed at the loudness and shock of it—not a light blush but a dark, red, flooding blush on her face and her neck that confused her and made her lower her head like a child caught stealing. She put her hands behind her back like a child. I blushed, too. She walked up and down a yard or two, her head still down, thinking. Then she walked away to the house.

"You'd better come inside," she called back in an offhand way.

You could have put our house into the hall and sitting-room of Heading Mount. I had been in that room when I was a boy, helping the waitress when my father was there doing the catering for a party. I do not know what you'd have to pay for the furniture there—thousands, I suppose. She led me through the room to a smaller room beyond it, where there was a desk. I felt I was slowly walking miles. I have never seen such a mess of papers and letters. They were even spread on the carpet. She sat down at the desk.

"Can you see the bill?" she muttered, not looking at me and pointing to the floor.

"I've got it here," I said, taking the bill out of my pocket. She jerked her head. The flush had gone, and now she looked as keen as needles at me.

"Well, sit down," she said.

She took the bill from me and looked at it. Now I could see that her skin was not white but was really pale and clay-coloured, with scores of little cracks in it, and that she was certainly nearer forty than thirty, as Mother always said.

"I've paid this," she said, giving the bill a mannish slap. "I pay every quarter."

"It has been running for three and a half years," I said, more at ease now.

"What?" she said. "Oh, well, I paid something, anyway. This isn't a bill. It's a statement."

"Yes," I said. "We have sent you the bills."

"Where's the date? This hasn't got any date on it."

I got up and pointed to the date.

"It ought to be at the top," she said.

My giddiness had gone. Noisy came into the room. "Hullo, Bob," he said. "I've just been talking to that beautiful thing you have got in the car." He always spoke in an alert, exhausted way about women, like someone at a shoot waiting for the birds to come over. "Have you seen Bob's girl, darling?" he said to her. "I've just offered her the key to my heart." And he lifted the silk scarf he was wearing in the neck of his canary-coloured pullover, and there was a piece of string round his neck with a heavy old door key hanging from it. Noisy gave a twitch to one side of his face.

"Oh, God, that old gag," said Mrs. Brackett.

"Not appreciated, old boy," said Noisy to me.

"Irresistible," said Mrs. Brackett, with an ugly mouth. She turned and spoke to me again, but glanced shrewdly at Noisy as she did so. "Let me try this one on you," she said. "You've already got my husband's cheques for this bill. I send him down to pay you, and he just cashes them?"

"I'm afraid not, Mrs. Brackett," I said. "That wouldn't be possible."

"You can't get away with that one, my pet," said Noisy. "Are you ready to go out?" He looked at her dress, admiring her figure. "What a target, Bob," he said.

"I don't think we will ask Mr. Fraser's opinion," she said coldly, but very pleased. And she got up and started out of the room, with Noisy behind her.

"You had better send me the bills," she called back to me, turning round from the door.

I felt very, very tired. I left the house and slammed the car door when I got in. "Now she wants the damn bills," I said to Rosie as I drove her up to Tolton station. I did not speak to her the rest of the way. She irritated me, sitting there.

*   *   *

When I got home and told my mother, she was short with me. That was the way to lose customers, she said. I was ruining all the work she and Dad had put into the business. I said if Mrs. Brackett wanted her bills she could come and get them herself. Mother was very shocked.

She let it go for a day or two, but she had to bring it up again. "What are you sulking about?" she said to me one afternoon. "You upset Rosie this morning. Have you done those bills for Mrs. Brackett yet?"

I made excuses, and got in the car and went over to

the millers and to the people who make our boxes, to get away from the nagging. Once I was out of the town, in the open country, Mrs. Brackett seemed to be somewhere just ahead of me, round a corner, over a hill, beyond a wood. There she was, trying to make me forget she owed us two hundred and twenty-eight pounds fourteen and fourpence. The moment she was in my head, the money went out of it. When I got back, late in the evening, Mother was on to me again. Noisy had been in. She said he had been sent down by his wife to ask why I had not brought the bills.

"The poor Wing Commander," my mother said. "Another rumpus up there." (She always gave him his rank if there was a rumour of another quarrel at Heading.) "She never gives him any peace. He's just an errand boy. She does what she likes with him."

"He's been offering you the key to his heart, Mother," I said.

"I don't take any stock of him," Mother said. "Or that pansy sweetheart stuff. Dad was the one and only for me. I don't believe in second marriages. I've no time for jealous women; they're always up to something, like Mrs. Doubleday thinking I spoke to her husband in the bank and she was caught with the chemist, but you always think the Fairy Prince will turn up—it's natural."

It always took a little time getting at what was in Mother's mind, yet it was really simple. She was a good churchwoman, and she thought Noisy was not really married to Mrs. Brackett, because he had been divorced by his first wife. She did not blame Noisy for this—in fact, she admired it, in a romantic way—but she blamed Mrs. Brackett, because, by Mother's theories, Mrs. Brackett was still single. And Mother

never knew whether to admire single women for holding
out or to suspect them of being on the prowl. One thing
she was certain of. "Money talks," she said. The thing
that made Noisy respectable for her, and as good as
being married in church, was that he had married Mrs.
Brackett for her money.

She talked like this the night we sat up and did that
month's bills, but the next day—and this was the
trouble with Mother—it ended in a row. I sent the bills
up to Mrs. Brackett by our delivery van.

"That is not the way to behave," Mother said. "You
should have taken them yourself."

And before the day was out, Mother was in a temper
again. Mrs. Brackett had spoken to her on the telephone
and said she had been through the bills and that we had
charged her for things she hadn't had, because she'd
been in the South of France at the time.

"I told you to go," Mother said to me.

I was angry, too, at being called dishonest. I got out
the van and said I was going up at once.

"Oh, that's how it is," said my mother, changing
round again. "Her Ladyship snaps her fingers and you
go up at once. She's got you running about for her like
Noisy. If I ask you to do anything, you don't pay any
attention to me. But Mrs. Brackett—she's the Queen of
England. Two of you running after her."

Mother was just like that with Father when he was
alive. He took no notice. Neither did I. I went up to
Heading. A maid let me in, and I sat there waiting in
the drawing-room. I waited a long time, listening to the
bees coming down the chimney, circling lower and
lower and then roaring out into the room, like Noisy's
car. I could hear Mrs. Brackett talking on the telephone
in her study. I could hear now and then what she was

saying. She was a great racing woman, and from words she said here and there I would say she was speaking to a bookmaker. One sentence I remember, because I think it had the name of a horse in it, and when I got back home later I looked up the racing news to see if I could find it. "Tray Pays On," she said. She came out into the room with the laughter of her telephone call still on her face. I was standing up, with our account book in my hand, and when she saw me the laughter went.

I was not afraid of her any more. "I hear there is some trouble about the bills," I said. "If you've got them, you can check them with the book. I've brought it."

Mrs. Brackett was a woman who watched people's faces. She put on her dutiful, serious, and obedient look, and led me again to the little room where the papers were. She sat down and I stood over her while we compared the bills and the book. I watched the moving of her back as she breathed. I pointed to the items, one by one, and she nodded and ticked the bills with a pencil. We checked for nearly half an hour. The only thing she said was in the middle of it—"You've got a double jointed thumb. So have I"—but she went right on.

"I can see what it is," I said at the end. "You've mistaken 1953 for '54."

She pushed the book away, and leaned back in the chair against my arm, which was resting on it.

"No, I haven't," she said, her small, unsmiling face looking up into mine. "I just wanted you to come up."

She gazed at me a long time. I thought of all the work Mother and I had done, and then that Mother was right about Mrs. Brackett. I took my hand from the chair and stepped back.

"I wanted to ask you one or two things," she said,

confidingly, "about that property next to the shop. I'll be fair with you. I'm interested in it. Are you? All right, don't answer. I see you are."

My heart jumped. Ever since I could remember, Father and Mother had talked of buying this property. It was their daydream. They simply liked little bits of property everywhere, and now I wanted it so that we could join the shop and the café.

"I asked because . . ." She hesitated. "I'll be frank with you. The bank manager was talking about it to me today."

My fright died down. I didn't believe that the bank manager—he was Mr. Pickering's brother-in-law—would let my mother down and allow the property to go to Mrs. Brackett without giving us the offer first.

"We want it, of course," I said. And then I suspected this was one of her tricks. "That is why I have been getting our bills in," I said.

"Oh, I didn't think that was it," she said. "I thought you were getting married. My husband says you are engaged to the girl you brought up here. He said he thought you were. Has she any money?"

"Engaged!" I said. "I'm not. Who told him that?"

"Oh," she said, and then a thought must have struck her. I could read it at once. In our town, if you cough in the High Street the chemist up at the Town Hall has got a bottle of cough mixture wrapped up and waiting for you; news travels fast. She must have guessed that when Noisy came down dangling the key to his heart, he could have been round the corner all the time, seeing Rosie.

"I'm glad to hear you're not engaged," Mrs. Brackett said tenderly. "I like a man who works. You work like your father did—God, what an attractive man!

You're like him. I'm not flattering you. I saw it when you came up the first time."

She asked me a lot of questions about the shop and who did the baking now. I told her I didn't do it and that I wanted to enlarge the restaurant. "The machine bakeries are getting more and more out into the country," I said. "And you've got to look out."

"I don't see why you shouldn't do catering for schools," she said. "And there's the Works." (Her father's main factory.) "Why don't you get hold of the catering there?"

"You can only do that if you have capital. We're not big enough," I said, laughing.

"How much do you want?" she said. "Two thousand? Three? I don't see why we couldn't do something."

The moment she said "we" I came to my senses. Here's a funny turnout, I thought. She won't pay her bills, but first she's after these shops, and now she's waving two thousand pounds in my face. Everyone in our town knew she was artful. I suppose she thought I was green.

"Not as much as two thousand," I said. "Just the bill," I said, nodding at it.

Mrs. Brackett smiled. "I like you. You're interested in money. Good. I'll settle it." And, taking her cheque book from the top of the desk, she put it in her drawer. "I never pay these accounts by cheque. I pay in cash. I'll get it tomorrow at the bank. I'll tell you what I'll do. You've got a shoe of mine. Bring it up tomorrow evening at, say, half past eight. I'll be back by then and you can have it." She paused, and then, getting up, added quickly, "Half tomorrow, half in October."

It was like dealing with the gypsies that come to your door.

"No, Mrs. Brackett," I said. "I'd like all of it. Now."
We stared at each other. It was like that moment
months ago when she had driven at me in her car and I
had reversed down the drive with one eye watching her
and one on the road as I shot back. That was the time, I
think, I first noticed her—when she opened her mouth
to shout a word at me and then did not shout. I could
have stayed like this, looking into her small, pretty,
miser's blue eyes, at her determined head, her chopped-
off fair hair, for half an hour. It was a struggle.

She was the first to speak, and that was a point gained
to me. Her voice shook a little. "I don't keep that
amount of money in the house," she said.

I knew that argument. Noisy said she always had two
or three hundred pounds in the safe in the wall of her
study, and whether this was so or not, I could not help
glancing toward it.

"I don't like being dictated to," she said, catching
my glance. "I have told you what I will do."

"I think you could manage it, Mrs. Brackett," I
said.

I could see she was on the point of flying into one of
her tempers, and as far as I was concerned (I don't
know why), I hoped she would. Her rows with Noisy
were so famous that I must have wanted to see one for
myself. And I didn't see why she should get away with
it. At the back of my mind, I thought of all the others
down in the town and how they would look when I said
I had got my money out of Mrs. Brackett.

Yet I wasn't really thinking about the money at all,
at this moment. I was looking at her pretty shoulders.

But Mrs. Brackett did not fly into a temper. She considered me, and then she spoke in a quiet voice that took
me off my guard. "Actually," she said, lowering her

29

eyes, "you haven't been coming up here after money at all, have you?"

"Well—" I began.

"Sh-h-h!" she said, jumping up from her chair and putting her hand on my mouth. "Why didn't you ring me and tell me you were coming? I am often alone."

She stepped to the door and bawled out, "Jimmy!" as if he were a long way off. He was—to my surprise, and even more to hers—very near.

"Yes, ducky?" Noisy called back from the hall.

"Damn," she said to me. "You must go." And, squeezing my hand, she went through the drawing-room into the hall.

"What time do we get back tomorrow evening?" she said boldly to Noisy. "Half past eight? Come at half past eight," she said, turning to me, for I had followed her. "I'll bring back the cash."

The sight of Noisy was a relief to me, and the sound of the word "cash" made Noisy brighten.

"Not lovely little bits of money!" he exclaimed.

"Not you," said Mrs. Brackett, glaring at him.

"How did you work it, old boy?" said Noisy later, giving me one of his most quizzical twitches as he walked with me to my van. When I drove off, I could see him still standing there, watching me out of sight.

I drove away very slowly. My mind was in confusion. About half a mile off, I stopped the car and lit a cigarette. All the tales I had heard about Mrs. Brackett came back into my mind. It was one thing to look at her, another thing to know about her. The one person I wished I had with me was Noisy. He seemed like a guarantor of safety, a protection. To have had my thoughts read like that by her filled me with fear.

I finished my cigarette. I decided not to go straight

home, and I drove slowly all along the lower sides of
the oak woods, so slowly and carelessly that I had to
swerve to avoid oncoming cars. I was making, almost
without knowing it, for the Green Man, at Mill Cross.
There was a girl there I had spoken to once or twice.
No one you would know. I went in and asked for a glass
of beer. I hardly said a word to her, except about the
weather, and then she left the bar to look after a baby in
the kitchen at the back. That calmed me. I think the way
she gave me my change brought me back to earth and
made me feel free of Mrs. Brackett's spell. At any rate, I
put the threepence in my pocket and swallowed my beer.
I laughed at myself. Mrs. Brackett had gypped me again.

*   *   *

When I got home, it was late, and my mother was
morose. She was wearing a black dress she often wore
when she was alone, dressed up and ready to go out, yet
not intending to, as if now that my father was dead she
was free if someone would invite her. Her best handbag
was beside her. She was often waiting like this, sitting on
the sofa, doing nothing but listening to the clock tick,
and perhaps getting up to give a touch to some flowers
on the table and then sitting down again. Her first words
shook me.

"Mrs. Brackett was down here looking for you," she
said sharply. "I thought you were with her. She wants
you to be sure to go up tomorrow evening to collect
some money when she comes back from Tolton. Where
have you been?"

"Let the old bitch post it or bring it in," I said.

Mother was horrified at the idea of Mrs. Brackett
soiling her hands with money.

"You'll do as I tell you," she said. "You'll go up and get it. If you don't, Noisy will get his hands on it first. You'd think a woman with all that money would go to a decent hairdresser. It's meanness, I suppose."

And then, of course, I saw I was making a lot of fuss about nothing. Noisy would be there when I went up to Heading. Good old Noisy, I thought; thank God for that. And he'll see I get the money, because she said it in front of him.

So the next evening I went. I put my car near the garage, and the first person I saw was Noisy, standing beside his own car. He had a suitcase in his hand. I went over to him.

"Fairy Queen's been at work," he said. He nodded at his tyres. They were flat. "I'm doing some quick thinking."

At that moment, a top window of the house was opened and someone emptied a suitcase of clothes out of it, and then a shower of cigarettes came down.

"She's tidying," he said. "I've got a quarter of an hour to catch the London train. Be a sweetie-pie and run me over there."

I had arrived once more in the middle of one of the Brackett rows. Only this time Noisy was leaving it to me. That is how I felt about it. "Hop in," I said.

And when we were off and a mile from Heading, he sat up in the seat and looked round. "Nothing on our tail," he said.

"Have you ever heard of a horse called Tray?" I asked him. "Tray Pays something? Tray Pays On— that can't be it."

"Tray Pays On?" repeated Noisy. "Is it a French horse?"

"I don't know," I said.

"Bloody peasant? Could be," said Noisy. "Sounds a bit frog to me."

We got to Tolton station. Noisy was looking very white and set with hatred. Not until he was standing in the queue getting his ticket did it occur to me what Noisy was doing.

"The first time I've travelled by train for fifteen years," he called to me across from the queue. "Damned serious. You can tell her if you see her"—people stared —"the worm has turned. I'm packing it in for good."

And as he went off to the train, he called, "I suppose you are going back? No business of mine, but I'll give you a tip. If you do, you won't find anything in the kitty, Bob." He gave me his stare and his final twitch. It was like the crack of a shot. Bang on, as he would have said. A bull's-eye.

I walked slowly away as the London train puffed out. I took his advice. I did not go back to Heading.

There were rows and rows between the Bracketts, but there was none like this one. It was the last. The others were a chase. This was not. For only Mrs. Brackett was on the road that night. She was seen, we were told, in all the likely places. She had been a dozen times through the town. Soon after ten o'clock she was hooting outside our house. Mother peeped through the curtains, and I went out. Mrs. Brackett got out of her car and marched at me. "Where have you been?" she shouted. "Where is my husband?"

"I don't know," I said.

"Yes, you do," she said. "You took him to Tolton, they told me."

"I think he's gone to London," I said.

"Don't be a damn liar," she said. "How can he have? His car is up there."

"By train," I said.

"By train," she repeated. Her anger vanished. She looked at me with astonishment. The rich are very peculiar. Mrs. Brackett had forgotten people travel by train. I could see she was considering the startling fact. She was not a woman to waste time staying in one state of mind for long. Noisy used to say of her, "That little clock never stops ticking."

"I see," she said to me sarcastically, nodding out the words. "That's what you and Jimmy have been plotting." She gave a shake to her hair and held her chin up. "You've got your money and you don't care," she said.

"What money is that?" I said.

"What money!" she exclaimed sharply, going over each inch of my face. What she saw surprised her at first. Until then she had been fighting back, but now a sly look came to her; it grew into a smile; the smile got wider and wider, and then her eyes became two curved lines, like crow's wings in the sky, and she went into shouts of laughter. It sounded all down the empty street. She rocked with it.

"Oh, no!" she laughed. "Oh, no, that's too good! That's a winner. He didn't give you a penny! He swiped the lot!"

And she looked up at the sky in admiration of that flying man. She was still grinning at me when she taunted breathlessly, "I mean to say—I mean to say—"

I let her run on.

"It was all or nothing with you, wasn't it?" she said. "And you get nothing, don't you?"

I am not sure what I did. I may have started to laugh it off and I may have made a step toward her. Whatever I did, she went hard and prim, and if ever a woman

34

ended anything, she did then. She went over to the car, got in, and slammed the door.

"You backed the wrong horse when you backed Jimmy," she called out to me.

That was the last of her. No more Mrs. Brackett at the shop. "You won't hear another word from her," my mother said.

"What am I supposed to do—get her husband back?" I said.

By the end of the week, everyone in the town was laughing and winking at me.

"You did the trick, boy," the grocer said.

"You're a good-looking fellow, Bob," the iron-monger said.

"Quite a way with the girls," the butcher said. "Bob's deep."

For when Mrs. Brackett went home that night, she sat down and paid every penny she owed to every shopkeeper in the town. Paid everyone, I say. Bar me.

NOISY FLUSHES THE BIRDS

2

Noisy Flushes the Birds

THINGS were quiet in the town; they'd been quiet for a year.

"You put on your clothes," Mother said one evening, after we had closed the shop, "and it isn't worth it." That hat she bought in Ainsworth, she said, the blue one—she'd only worn it once.

But it was September now and, in our part of the country, if anything happens, September is the time for it. The harvest is in, people have nothing to do, except think of how they can annoy one another. I have heard holiday visitors put this down to the strong air, the variable warm Atlantic winds that send us half asleep so that we don't know whether we are alive or dreaming; Miss Croggan, the headmistress of the girls' school, says it's the Celtic blood taking time off to stir up old feuds. But nothing had happened, so far, this year. There was nothing to compare, for example, with the week Teddy Longfellow introduced two lunatics to the town and persuaded Major Dingle—Nigerian police, retired, and a stickler for the "right people"—that they were a pair of baronets looking for a large property in the neighbour-hood. The year before that, there was Hoblin, the farmer, who used disguised voices on the telephone, pretending that he was the Chief Constable, an official from the Ministry of Agriculture, the County Medical Officer, and so on, inquiring into a report that Teddy Longfellow had been watering his milk; he kept the story up for days, until Teddy nearly pulled his red beard off with panic.

And to move from fiction to fact, we had had no scandal to match the break-up of the Brackett marriage. No Bentleys about at night, I mean. No Noisy Brackett roaring through the town, followed a few minutes later by his wife chasing him. Their married life had been, for us, like one of those air displays when suddenly a pair of jets scream the place down, vanish into a whistle and, then, silence; suddenly, five minutes later, they are back again, down your neck, like wasps. Mother and I closed the shop in the evening, as I say, and we sat down doing nothing.

"Can't you talk?" she said. "Your father used to."

"I've been on my legs all day," I said.

Like an enormous, simple-minded cheese the September moon came slowly over the houses opposite and we stared at it. The size of it, Mother said, upset her.

And then—as if the moon had started them off—things began to happen. One thing after another. I caught it first. I went out to a dance on the Saturday night and, driving back, I got engaged to a girl called Claudia Dingle. I knew before I went that it was ten to one I would get engaged to someone or other. Claudia was the daughter of Major Dingle up at the Old Rectory, the man Teddy Longfellow had made a fool of. She was a tall girl with a small cloudy head of golden hair that seemed to be blowing off her head like flame, yet with a voice as cool as a water ice. She was so slight that I thought she would snap in two when she laughed. She had just come back from a finishing school in Switzerland. You should have heard the band play up at the Old Rectory and at our house, too! Mother pretended not to hear first of all when I told her and then said "Every time you go to a dance you get engaged." When I said "Only twice," Mother said:

"They don't get their bread from us; they deal with Higgs." Up at Claudia's house the Major said:

"That hulking lad who comes round the back door with the bread and works in the café! Is the girl out of her mind?"

"Anyway," said Claudia on the second day, "it'll be divine to work in the shop. And you don't always have to be a baker."

"Actually, my sweet," I said, putting on a drawling voice like hers, "I do."

She said she didn't mean it that way. She said it wasn't her fault she was upper class and she'd adore to go out in the van with me.

Any time I got engaged it always upset me. It upset other people, too, and Mother got moody; and Claudia had no tact either, coming in and out of the shop and wanting to look at the bakehouse and saying how divine it was, when we were busy, and upsetting the girls. But the thing that set Mother against her was saying she was going to have the announcement put in *The Times*. Mother thought she meant the *County Times* and so did I, but Claudia meant the London *Times*.

"Everyone does," Claudia said.

"I never heard of it in this town yet," I said. "I'd look a damn fool."

Mother said it was daft; no one in the town would know. I argued this with Claudia.

"I meant *people*, not the town," said Claudia. She didn't mean any harm; her finishing school had finished her.

The announcement went into the London *Times*.

* * *

One evening when I had been out at her house I came back home early and Mother was sitting at the window.

"What are you sitting there for; you can't see to read," I said to her.

"Troubling about me—that is new," Mother said. "I've had my life." And then she said, changing her voice to something like Mrs. Dingle's refined accents, and mocking:

"We've had another of your old lady friends in this afternoon—Mrs. Brackett. It never rains but it pours."

My heart gave a jump like a fish.

"What did she want—credit?" I said.

"She's asked you and this girl—what is her name?—Claudia—to dinner," said my mother. "She asked me. No, I said, not me. I never go out, not since Dad died." Mother thought eating with anyone but our relations a wickedness and only went to their houses because it was painful; and she looked like the Ten Commandments at anyone else who invited her to go out.

"She read about it in that London paper," Mother said, accusing Claudia and me. And then we had the usual line about making your bed and lying on it.

"You can go and see the nobs if you like," she said. "And feast yourself on all this getting engaged and getting divorced. Dad was the one and only for me and we were true. You think you want the Fairy Prince, it's womanlike—but it's all soft pansy nonsense. I blame *her*; you don't know whether she's married or single; lady she may call herself, but I don't see she's even a woman, not a real woman." And Mother added: "She's got stout."

The women in our town got stout or thin from day to day, according to Mother's moods. Father used to say he never knew a town where the weight and measurements of women changed so often and where an ordinary dress or coat was ever of the right length.

42

I switched on the light and I saw Mother's face looking square and offended, suspicion puffing it out. I expected her to look sulky, but I was astonished to see it was worse than that. She looked insulted and miserable.

"She paid her bill," Mother said bitterly. She might have been looking at her grave in the churchyard. She was also suspicious.

"We had a long chat," Mother said. "She came inside." (Mother referred to the room at the back of the shop which was a mixture of sitting-room, store-room and office. When Mother came out of it with anyone who had been "asked inside" she always had a peculiar look on her face—pleased and unnatural. You could never get her to say what "they" had said.)

I was as surprised as Mother that Mrs. Brackett had paid. And I was suspicious, too.

"After five years, about time, too," I said. "I wonder what put that idea into her head?" I said.

"Why ask me?" said Mother. "I'm not getting engaged to all these girls; you were the one chasing after her, driving her husband out of the house."

"Chasing after Mrs. Brackett!" I said.

Mother was on to her old tale. You won't believe it, but she blamed me for Mrs. Brackett's divorce! Just because I ran into Noisy Brackett that evening a year before and he asked me to give him a lift to the station. How did I know he was leaving his wife?

We sat saying nothing.

"Well," said Mother, "you've come in. Haven't you any news?"

*   *   *

News! We had it next day in the lunch hour when the

shop was closed. I was eating a chop when something went by with a roar. I mean something in the street. There was a screech at the sharp left bend at the Church and then a noise like someone tumbling dustbins over. I put my knife and fork down.

"Sit down," said Mother, getting up herself and going to the window. "That's Noisy Brackett. He's back."

Mother was holding the curtains. She was lit up with excitement. Even her brown hair shone.

"I knew he'd come back," she cried. And she touched her hair here and there and brushed the crumbs off her dress.

"If it's Noisy he's hit something," I said, getting up again.

"Sit down," she said. She turned on me in a temper.

"People leave cars all over this town, no wonder there are accidents. The police ought to stop it," she shouted.

Mother had always thought that all cars should be cleared out of the town so that Noisy Brackett could have a clear run through at ninety miles an hour. Mother smiled again. She was in heaven. If it had been anyone else but Noisy she would have screamed, pushed me to the door, pulled me back—but not for Noisy. He was a god; he could do anything.

I didn't believe it was Noisy; I think I know a Bentley when I hear one. But when I went up the street I found out Mother was right. People were still looking at the tyre marks on the street and the pavement. A couple of shopkeepers were looking at the back doors of their vans that had been cannoned down the hill. It was Noisy, they said. He had gone off now, nobody knew where. But the police, of course, had got him somewhere outside the town.

At first Mother was upset that Noisy had gone clean through the town without stopping for a word with us. But when Mother heard that he had been summoned for dangerous driving she was in Paradise. He would be back! He would be up before the Court. And if any of those stuffed animals on the Bench dared to do anything to her Noisy she would put arsenic in their bread, she would tell their wives all she knew, and so on. But, underneath and more powerful, her feeling was different. You have got to know Mother. Noisy was back. That meant, for her, that "they"—Mrs. Brackett and Noisy —were reconciled. The divorce was off. "*He* loved *Her*." He was back in Heading, that beautiful house, full of those things worth thousands, life was normal; love— "the one and only"—was triumphant after all. And, to crown it, that dear sweet girl Claudia and I were invited there to dinner at the very throne of matrimonial happiness, an object lesson to us all. In the week following my engagement and Noisy's summons to appear in court on a charge of "wanton driving to the public danger" I have not known Mother so suddenly turn to happiness since Father's death.

All the same, Mrs. Brackett did not turn up at the court when Noisy's case came on. Mother was a bit put out by this when I told her, but she said that it never looks nice when women are mixed up in the law; her own father left it in his will that no woman should go to his funeral. But I'll tell you who did turn up—I mean aside from half the town, and someone from the Ainsworth Press—Teddy Longfellow. He was Noisy's witness. He had been in the car at the time. Teddy was a funny man. He had a loud reddish suit on, with yellow squares on it, but it was not that—people said he got himself up to look like Satan. It was the way his hair came to a point in front and stood up in a couple of horns at the sides; and his beard. It was his stammer that made people say he had been a German spy.

But we had come to look at Noisy, to see how he would get out of it. The police had got him thoroughly tied up. There he was, the same old Noisy. Small, thin— "his poor chest", Mother used to say—with a head of oily crinkly black hair, his gypsyish skin and always the dandy. He was all nerves and illness in an electric way and the women loved him for that. And there was that sudden twitch to one side of his face. It pulled the skin down from the eye, which seemed to stare out from the middle of calamity like the end of a pistol, before his face went back into dozens of soft smiling wrinkles. We knew he'd get off somehow, but how we could not imagine. He denied, of course, that he was doing fifty, because, as he said, he knew that corner by heart. And Teddy Longfellow denied it also.

"I was practically at a standstill, sir," Noisy said to the Bench, with a shocked, polite glance at the police. "But an extraordinary thing happened. I've never known it happen before in twenty-five years of driving; Le Mans, Monte Carlo, Brooklands. I sneezed, sir, just on the turn. A blinding sneeze, sir, without warning, quite extraordinary, like an explosion, like a bomb flash. Visibility absolutely nil. I didn't know where I was. I lost control. Never done it before. It was a mercy I was only doing twenty-two at the time, as Teddy, I mean the witness has just said. Perhaps I ought to say I suffer from hay fever. I got it in India."

And when he said "sneeze" Noisy's face gave one of his twitches and sudden stares with his left eye, as if he were going to produce a sample sneeze in court, a final burst, to make sure. The Chairman even started to raise

46

his hand to ward it off. Well, the Bench hummed and ha'ed, but, of course, Noisy got off. Afterwards, at the Red Lion, he did one or two of these sneezes to show us; one of his Squadron Leaders during the war, he said, could do it with a monocle in his eye, without dropping it.

"I must pop in and have a word with your mama, Bob," Noisy said to me. And when he came to the shop he gave Mother a kiss and said:

"What's happened? You look ten years younger, Mrs. Fraser. I wonder if you would add to all your kindnesses and cash me a teeny weeny little cheque. Yes? You're quite sure? Now, isn't that like old times?"

"Come inside," Mother said, blushing with happiness, leading him to the room at the back. "I'm ashamed of you." They stayed inside talking quite a while and when they came out Mother's face was blissful.

"Now remember your promise! Go and see," said my mother, and she walked with him to the doorstep of the shop.

"I will. You bet I will, Mrs. Fraser. Bang on." Noisy smiled and waved to her. I walked a few yards with him. His face changed, he gave a serious twitch and said, in a dead, quizzing voice:

"How is she? How's the Fairy Queen? Have you seen her?"

"Not to speak to," I said.

He looked as though he didn't quite believe me.

"I hear she paid her bill," he said.

"Yes," I said.

"Lovely money," he said. "I've got a spot of trouble there. Keep it under your hat—she's got her tiny little hands on my birds. She won't give them up. You don't

48

know my birds! Yes, you do. That big case of birds that stands inside the door at Heading. Tropical birds. They're mine."

I didn't remember them. Heading was so full of things.

"She can have what she likes, but she's not going to have my birds," said Noisy. "I'm going to get them. I've got to. I've sold them. I need the cash." Noisy's face was now hard and serious; he lit a cigarette and wagged it up and down on his lips, studying my van. "Wonderful woman, the Fairy Queen, really one of the best. But there's going to be a burglary."

We got to his car and Teddy Longfellow was there.

"Take a look at this. T'that's what we w'want," Teddy said. He was nodding to our van, which was parked behind his car. "Take out the shelves and Bob's your uncle."

"Hear that?" said Noisy to me. "He's a natural car thief, that's how he made all his money. See you one of these days." They got into Noisy's car, Noisy turned to give a tremendous sneeze for my benefit, there was the lovely throb of his engine and he was off.

You pass Teddy Longfellow's house on the Ainsworth road. It stands on a hill, one of those modern houses of glass and steel with a spiral staircase enclosed in a glass tower in front and something like the top of a lighthouse on the roof. It was built just as the war broke out and people said Longfellow had built it so that he could signal to the Germans from it. Claudia and I drove past once or twice and I was telling her that Teddy had made a fortune out of cotton and was a damn good farmer, the only up-to-date farmer in the district. I started telling her about the two fake baronets he had introduced to the town. The place, I said, is full of snobs.

Of course, there I put my foot in it. I'd clean forgotten that Claudia's father, the Major, had been Teddy's victim. Class is a funny thing. Claudia was a pretty girl, no brain as Mother said, I give you that; but sweet and she stood up to the old Major and her mother with a will of her own; but when it came to class and family—well, she was her mother all over again. I've seen it since. I got the lot. Teddy was not a gentleman; he was just a shot-up businessman—at the word "business" her face went sick—pretending to be a county gentleman and trying to buy his way in. He was loud. He was vulgar. He was rude. Of course, he wasn't a German, but loads of Germans came to visit him after the war. They came, Claudia said, to look at his pictures.

"They're worth a lot, aren't they?" I said.

"You're always talking about money," Claudia said.

"It's what I live on," I said.

"I don't know how much they're worth," said Claudia. "And I'm not interested. I only know my parents took Mrs. Brackett over there one day and she proved to him his big Cézanne was fake. He's never forgiven her."

"Cézanne—who's he?" I said.

"French, a painter," she said. "A very great painter."

"Oh," I said. "Must be, if he's a friend of Mrs. Brackett's. I'm ignorant."

As I say, she was a sweet girl; you couldn't blame her. We had a bit of a quarrel on the way home. She told me her father had tried to stop her from driving with me on the bread round. He told her she was breaking the law, because of the licence. Of course, Mrs. Dingle had put the Major up to that. I, like a fool, not thinking, said I'd often taken our girls out in it, the girls from the shop.

"And Mrs. Brackett, I suppose," said Claudia sulkily.

"Old Mrs. B., the Fairy Queen!" I said. "I'm not a bloody fool."

"She's not old," said Claudia.

"No, I suppose she isn't," I said. "She *looks* young. Very young sometimes."

"Young!" exclaimed Claudia. "Thirty-eight—I don't call that young."

That was another thing my father used to say about the women of our town. They changed their age faster than in any other place he had ever known. A woman might be thirty in the morning and fifty-five by six in the evening or vice versa.

"Like bread," he used to say. "You see it rise, then it goes flat."

*　　*　　*

The last thing I wanted to do was to go to have dinner with Mrs. Brackett. The idea that just because I was engaged to Claudia Dingle I had to be paraded before the friends of her family, and Mrs. Brackett above all, preyed on my mind. I had scarcely seen Mrs. Brackett for a year, not since the time she came down to our house shouting and asking what I'd done with her husband. I had kept out of her way. Claudia was dragging me into this and I couldn't help saying to Mother: "That's the last time I get engaged at a dance."

"It is," said Mother. "Who's in a mood now?"

But the day before the dinner I was walking up the town and just as I got to the garage petrol pumps I saw Mrs. Brackett. I was going to dodge into the paper shop, but I went on because I saw at once something was happening. Something that nearly made me laugh out loud. I had caught Mrs. Brackett on the point of cheating the garage hand. It was the prettiest sight in the world. She had just had a gallon of petrol put in her car and the garage hand—it was Johnny Gibbs—was standing there with her money in his open hand and telling her that the price was a penny more. She was cocking an eyebrow at him, which she well knew how to do, and gave a glance up and down the street. She was beginning to blush. Then she saw me. She turned her back on Johnny and came slowly towards me, like a cat. She was a small woman and I felt the old empty feeling I always had when I saw her walk; that she was going to dawdle her way clean through me.

"Hullo, stranger," she said in a pleased, ringing, boyish voice. "I've been in twice to congratulate you, but you weren't there." Mother had not told me about the second time.

Mrs. Brackett held out her hand. It was a small, square hand and strong; Claudia's hands were long and limp and you could feel the bones in them.

I didn't say much. I didn't know what to say.

"I'm glad you've shaved off your moustache," she said, looking me over. She had pretty blue eyes.

Even I noticed that Mrs. Brackett had altered. She still had something of the impudent twelve-year-old boy about her, but a boy who had tidied himself up. In Noisy's time she looked like what they call a "young varmint", with her hair chopped as if she had cut it herself, her red check shirt and her dusty old jeans and the lipstick always hit or miss. Now she was wearing a dress, terrible colours, of course—geranium with yellow flowers on it—but a dress and smart shoes and she had been to the hairdresser's. And she had got her figure down. I don't say she looked pretty, because the

bones of her face were too strong, but she looked alive.
And something else—I couldn't make it out. When I
said this to Mother, later on, Mother said:

"It's the divorce. Mrs. Gordon was the same when
she was divorced. She's trying to look respectable and
sort of sad. A woman has to think."

That wasn't my idea of Mrs. Brackett. I thought she
looked more like a woman, I mean one with a brain.

"Thanks for settling the bill," I said. I wanted to
show her I had won in the end and that I was glad all
that nonsense was over.

Mrs. Brackett didn't like that. She flushed. And she
bent forward her head and studied her shoes for quite a
while. Her dress was cut very low. Then she looked up
quickly and caught me looking.

"Weddings are expensive," she said, very cool. I
laughed.

"The bride's parents pay," I said.

Mrs. Brackett gave a shake to her head, as if a bullet
had whizzed near her.

"I bet you've told Claudia that," she said, mocking
me, but she was laughing. "You are a one, aren't you?"
And her little eyes closed into slits of glee as she
laughed.

"Tomorrow night," she said. She stepped into her
car and she was off.

Johnny Gibbs stood there with his hand open. Both
of us watched her go up the town and then stared at
each other; he was damn nearly accusing me of plotting
robbery.

Claudia was hanging about for me at home and when
she had gone Mother said:

"Why are you so rude to that poor girl? What is the
matter with you?"

"You heard her," I said. "She's trying to improve me," for I had told them about meeting Mrs. Brackett, and Claudia had been asking what I was going to wear. I had led her on and she was frightened I was just going to walk out of the bakehouse at seven o'clock in my overalls covered in flour and go up to Heading as I was.

"Why have I got to go up there anyway?" I said to Mother.

"The gardens are beautiful. Dad and I used to go up every spring when the rhododendrons were out. They'll take you round the gardens," said Mother, daydreaming.

"You keep on saying 'they'—I bet you anything you like Noisy won't be there," I said. "And it's September —the rhododendrons were over four months ago."

"You needn't be rude to me," Mother said. "He will be there. He promised me."

I told her about Johnny Gibbs and the penny.

"She's always up to something," I said.

"I bet she is," said Mother gaily. "You take up with the nobs and get yourself engaged. What d'you expect? Dad and I were content to be in business."

"Ah," I said, remembering. "That's a word Claudia doesn't like. Teddy Longfellow's in *business*. She doesn't like that."

"There's a lot of things girls don't like they have to get used to," said Mother.

But Mother was as agitated as I was, when the day for Mrs. Brackett's party came. One of her suspicious moods set in. It began with her suspecting the cash register and the bills for flour; she suspected one of the waitresses at our café; women who came into the shop began to put on weight—always a bad sign with Mother—and the colours of their clothes didn't suit them. The men looked shifty, she said; she didn't like a bank manager who drank and she was furious that the butcher opposite was having his shop painted—what a time of year! She was sharp with the girls at the shop— Rosie, the dark one, was almost in tears—and all three girls kept half-turning their heads and walked about round-shouldered because they knew Mother was watching them. If I came out of the bakery into the office or the shop, Mother stopped serving and watched me, too. The worst of all was that she suddenly did not trust Noisy.

"He's a man," she said.

"They're out for what they can get, both of them," she said. She suddenly remembered Mrs. Brackett had once talked of buying the property next door to us and she was glad anyway that we had stepped in and bought it a few months before.

"There is always a plot between those two," she said.

"You didn't tell me Mrs. Brackett had been in twice," I said.

"I did," said Mother. "Are you starting calling everyone a liar? Even your own Mother!"

I didn't think of it at the time—I never did think until after these moods were over—but I remember Dad used to say to her when she was like this:

"What's on your conscience, Mother?"

I'll come to that later.

Still she made an effort when I picked up Claudia at the Old Rectory and brought her back to show to Mother. Claudia was wearing a pale blue dress and her hair was cloudy and lovely. Mother wiped a tear at the sight of her and she was laughing when we waved goodbye; but when I turned back I saw Mother's face looking black with wretchedness as if she had seen us off to our execution or that we had left her to hers. I had

the terrible feeling that we were off to the other side of
the world and would never see her again and I blamed
Claudia for this.

It was a light evening with a mackerel sky, the
glimmer of the moon beginning on the stubble, and
glinting on the heavy trees and the warm air smelled of
the harvest. I was telling Claudia what the Government
subsidy meant to the farmers who were complaining,
though, for a fact, I could name three who had ten
thousand in the bank . . .

"Look," said Claudia interrupting. A soft owl flew
over the lane.

"And that's not counting Teddy Longfellow," I said.
"He must be worth a quarter of a million."

"When you used to come up here to see the Bracketts
was Rosie the one you took with you?" Claudia asked.
"The poor girl has got spots."

"I took her to see her brother," I said. "I think it was
her brother."

"Oh, look," said Claudia, "another owl. They're like
ghosts." And took her hand from mine. She was a
jealous girl.

But we were at Heading, driving through the deep
walls of rhododendrons.

What a change: not in the house itself—it was a long
L-shaped stone house with a wing making the angle—
but in the garden. The lawn in front was rough; the
mower had not been over it for months; one of the two
climbing roses that had spread along the building had
fallen off in a heap that entangled the flower-beds. They
had not been weeded or touched—all so trim and well
looked after in Noisy's time—but now let go. There was
a stack of logs beside the wide front door, no one had
bothered to move them in. Mrs. Brackett's car, in need

of a wash, stood near, and there was a station wagon not far from it.

"Whose is that?" I asked.

Claudia didn't know.

We went into the house. The door was open and Claudia called out. We were in the wide hall room that went to the back of the house. Then a tall, fair-haired man with a broken nose and wearing plimsolls came out of the drawing-room.

"Hullo," he said. "My name's Fobham, not that it matters. They're upstairs having a jaw."

It was Lord Fobham. He lived at Abbey Moor. He took Claudia's coat and then said something to me that I didn't hear. I was standing there staring. For—against the wall, was Noisy's case of birds. It was about four feet high, mounted on a stand, and contained a strange collection of stuffed birds perched on branches—birds of paradise, a pair of parrots, a golden pheasant, an oriole, an Indian kingfisher—so Lord Fobham said later. I was gaping at them. I was thinking Noisy must be mad to suppose he could walk in and lift a case like that.

"Awfully pretty. Victorian," said Lord Fobham to me. He had a busy manner, never standing still, as if he were shaking his bones up.

"It must weigh a lot," I said.

"Take a couple of footmen to lift it," said Lord Fobham.

"I didn't mean weigh," I said, confused. "I mean they must be worth a bit." Claudia bit her lip.

"No, don't think so, twenty-five quid the lot, no more. You pick them up anyway," said Lord Fobham briskly. Claudia said, to put me in my place:

"They're beautiful. They're priceless."

"You mean collectors after them?" said Lord

Fobham, getting interested in Claudia. "What would they give for a case like that?" Claudia studied them. She gave a severe glance at me and said:

"You'd better ask my father—but I'd say a hundred pounds."

"I'd give a hundred and fifty pounds," I said to annoy her.

"What!" said Lord Fobham, getting keen. "You mean that?" Lord Fobham was always selling off bits of family property, pictures and heirlooms. At this Mrs. Brackett and Lady Fobham came downstairs.

"What's this lot worth, Sally?" said Lord Fobham. "Mr. Fraser will give you a hundred for it."

"It was me," said Claudia.

"I wouldn't take three," said Mrs. Brackett.

"Well," said Lord Fobham to me, "if it's worth that to her I bet you'd easily find an American who'd give you twice that. What about your cousin?" he said to his wife.

"Don't be silly. He hasn't got a penny," said Lady Fobham. "It would smash if you moved it."

"Don't be a damn fool. Pack it properly, case it up. Like we did with all that china," said Lord Fobham to his wife. "Use your brain. Look. It's light." And he put his hands under the stand to tilt it.

"Come and have a drink and have a look at the other lots before you make up your mind," said Mrs. Brackett sarcastically.

"Damn funny. I never knew it, did you?" said Lord Fobham to me, looking back covetously at the case as we went into the drawing-room. "Probably worth eight hundred pounds."

"Where did you get it from?" he called to Mrs. Brackett.

"It was my father's," said Mrs. Brackett.

"Darling," said Lady Fobham. "He'd sell me."

"No offers," said Lord Fobham. "Are you in the business?" he said eagerly to me.

"No, Mr. Fraser's a baker," said Mrs. Brackett.

"Ah, you can tell me," said Lord Fobham, "something I've always wanted to know. Why can't I get a decent crust on a loaf nowadays? Bread never has any crust."

"Go to Mr. Fraser and you'll get all the crust you want," said Mrs. Brackett, going over to Claudia. "Darling, what a pretty dress. What are you drinking?"

"Ha! Ha! Ha!" Lady Fobham laughed. "Are you a baker? What fun! I thought bakers were little men. You're as tall as my husband."

"Taller. Use your eyes," said Lord Fobham to his wife. "God, how much gin did you put in this, Sally?" Mrs. Brackett talked to me.

"Gosh, she's pretty. Gosh, she's young," she said. "You know how to pick them. Have you known each other long?"

"Why does your father stuff his birds?" Lord Fobham was saying to Claudia. "I always shoot 'em."

"He doesn't stuff birds," said Claudia.

"Oh," said Lord Fobham. "Where does he shoot? Not up at Teddy Longfellow's, I hope. He shot a fox." And to me he said: "I always ask Sally about the gin— she waters it."

"I do think Sally's wonderful about clothes," said Lady Fobham to me, when Mrs. Brackett poured out more drinks. "She's got the most marvellous lack of colour sense I ever saw—tomato red—it's her personality brings it off. How do you do it, Sally?

"It's easy," said Mrs. Brackett. "I don't wear anything underneath."

"Really!" said Lady Fobham.

59

"No one to speak to Alice," Lord Fobham commanded, jerking a thumb at his wife. "A couple of martinis and she goes middle class."

I don't know how long we sat there. In spite of what Lord Fobham said the drinks were not watered this evening. They were strong. We went at last to dine in the large kitchen. Mrs. Brackett rarely had servants. Lord Fobham poured the wine.

"Oh, how lovely. The '53," said Claudia, clapping her hands and nodding to me. "Look," she said to me.

"It was the '51 I poured over Noisy," said Mrs. Brackett.

"Sally," said Lord Fobham, who had drunk quite a lot. "I never liked him."

"You're wrong there," said Mrs. Brackett. "*I* liked him a lot. Mr. Fraser likes Noisy, don't you?"

She looked at me innocently. I started to tell them about the way Noisy sneezed in court, but a look from Claudia showed me I ought not to have begun it. I went on all the same. But they were all beginning to shout.

"He's trying to tell a story. Everyone keep quiet," said Lady Fobham kindly, flashing rings at me.

"I can't see it," said Lord Fobham to me when I had done. "You mean he sneezed his hands off the wheel. He was plastered."

"I sneeze very loudly," said Claudia, helping.

"You ask yourself," said Lord Fobham, picking out a large potato from a dish and adding, "Go on, pick one yourself," to his wife. "You ask yourself what makes a man attractive to a woman . . ."

"No one asked," said Lady Fobham.

"Claudia knows," said Mrs. Brackett.

Lord Fobham poured the wine. We were making a terrible noise.

"All I can say . . ." Lord Fobham said. "All I can say . . ." but he couldn't get a word in edgeways.

"All you can say—what?" said Lady Fobham.

"Why are your kitchen chairs so hard?" he said to Mrs. Brackett. "My bottom's got points on it. No", he went on. "All I can say is I'm not like Teddy Long-fellow, an atheist, reads Darwin, thinks you can go to bed with any man's wife. I believe in humility."

"What!" cried Mrs. Brackett. "Humble—you!"

"I said humility," said Lord Fobham drunkenly. "Not humble. Don't be so damn middle class. There's a difference."

"There's no place like home," Lady Fobham began to sing, but stopped. "Why are you looking so surprised, all of you?"

Everyone became quiet. There was a silence broken only by the sound of the coffee-pot sizzling. There were candles on the table. The curtains were not drawn. Outside the night was dark. The mackerel sky had thickened.

Presently Mrs. Brackett said in a conversational voice:

"There's a man looking through the window." We had drunk so much that we all laughed together.

"A man," said Lady Fobham. "How nice."

"Through the end window," said Mrs. Brackett.

"I don't blame him," said Lord Fobham. "I went to dine with a fellow in Rio and half-way through dinner his wife said 'There's a man walking round the ceiling'. You're plastered, Sally."

"I'm tight, but I'm not plastered," said Mrs. Brackett. We all turned to look at the windows. There was nothing to see, but by her voice I knew Mrs. Brackett was not joking.

"I'll go and look," I said and left the room. I went

out in the passage, through a large farm scullery to the back door and out into the garden. This part of the garden was sheltered by a high yew hedge and the light from the dining-room lit it fairly well. The night was dark. I was in the shadow, but I could see no one. I was just going inside again when I saw what looked like a large dog jump to the hedge. I went across to look. No sign of a dog. I went right up to the hedge: it was too dense for any dog to get through. And then, as I moved, I trod on something soft. I looked down and there was a man lying under the hedge with his hands hiding his head. I was treading on him. I stepped back.

"Get up," I said.

But before I knew what to do, the man jumped to his feet and paused to stare. That curly hair, that twitch to the face was unmistakable. It was Noisy. He gave a leap and ran to the gate and was out of the garden before I could do anything. I didn't know what to do. Then I shouted to him. My shout brought out Lord Fobham and Mrs. Brackett, too.

"Who was it?" she said.

"I don't know," I said. "He looked like a gypsy."

"Get after him," they cried. So I ran and I could see Noisy dodging along the shadows of the barns; he vaulted a five-barred gate and into the field beyond it. I let him, of course; anyway, though I've got long legs I've never been much of a runner. Noisy was small, he sprinted fast. I got to the last lot of outbuildings and Mrs. Brackett was coming up, shouting "Where is he?"

"He's over the gate and into the field," I said. In fact, I had not seen where he went.

Mrs. Brackett and I started for the field, when we heard a car starting up on the other side of the house. "That's Bertie Fobham," said Mrs. Brackett, climbing

over the gate, but at that very moment Lord Fobham came walking up to us.

Mrs. Brackett had been grinning so far. She loved a hunt. But at this sound of a car driving off and with Lord Fobham beside us her grin went and a look of excited awakeness came to her boyish face.

"Quick," she said, pulling me by the coat. We started back. She rushed back through the yard and garden to the house and through it. And then we both stopped. The front door was wide open and where Mrs. Brackett's case of birds had stood there was now only the stand.

"It's Noisy. He's got them," said Mrs. Brackett.

"He can't have done it alone," I said.

We rushed out on to the drive. Lord Fobham's car was there and so was hers.

"Get in," she said. "Bertie's a dead loss. I bet he's in the water butt."

Far away, a good three-quarters of a mile across the flat fields, we could see the red tail-light of a car turn into the main road and its headlights fan northwards.

"There are two cars," I said, pointing to the splashes of light on the trees.

Mrs. Brackett was a fast driver. We were out of the long deep drive between the rhododendrons, past the estate cottages and in a little more than a minute were going northward on the winding road. Sometimes we saw the tail-light of the other car, sometimes we saw lights daubing the trees. There is a cross-roads not far off and when we were a quarter of a mile off we saw the car turn. As it turned it was picked out by the light of another car which turned in the opposite direction.

"There you are, two. That's our van," I said. Distinctly I saw our green van.

"What is our van doing up here?"

Mrs. Brackett did not answer. She had the racing instinct. Given a choice between chasing a van and a racing car, she chose the latter. At the cross-roads we let the van go. There is a high ridge of open common with a narrow, bumpy but straight road rising and falling for miles, running through scattered coppices of ghostly beeches, leaning and flattened, although we were far inland, by the Atlantic winds. The little dot of light in the distance led us on.

"That's Noisy," she said. I said nothing. I was sure it wasn't.

For Mrs. Brackett it must have been like the old days, the revival of those fierce pursuits of her married life. Her cheek bones were set, her eyes were happy. The wind blew her hair back and I saw her strong straight forehead; and all the time she drove, she was turning her head and talking to me, but in an inspired way, keeping an eye on the leaping road.

"Where did you meet Claudia?" she said as the needle rose steadily on the speedometer. "At a dance, I see. Which dance? When was that? And then you took her home? Is that when you got engaged? In the car? How old is she? Gosh, she's young."

I answered the questions. Suddenly Mrs. Brackett turned her head and came out with a blunt question.

"You're not in love with her, are you?" she said. "All right, you don't want to talk about it. I don't think you are in love with her. They've no money, you know."

"I'm not interested in money," I said violently.

"Keep your hair on," she said. Her voice changed and became nervous. "You don't like me, do you? All right, don't answer that one. When are you going to be married?"

"Not for a long time," I said to stop her talking.

"I think you're wise," she said. "It'd be unfair on her. We're gaining."

And we were. The other car was not more than half a mile ahead. I had been trying to get a real sight of it for a long time. I was trying to think whose car it was for I was convinced that Noisy was in our van, though how he had got it unless, of course, he had pitched some tale to Mother, I couldn't imagine.

"We've got him," said Mrs. Brackett and, in her excitement, squeezed my hand. I squeezed hers. Almost at once, the engine spluttered, our speed died. Within fifty yards we stopped and the other car was away over the brow of the next hill.

The silence of the country flowed in on us.

"Well?', said Mrs. Brackett.

"Sorry," I said and let Mrs. Brackett's hand go. I don't know why I had held it.

"Thank you," said Mrs. Brackett, taking her hand away. No petrol. It was the old story: Mrs. Brackett was too mean to fill up her car. It had happened over and over again in her pursuits of Noisy. We all knew it. I smiled. She looked small, indignant and surprised, like a child. We sat there staring on the dead road, in the night silence of the Common, listening to the engine cool and to the small movements of animals in the gorse.

"Bad luck," said Mrs. Brackett. "Damn." She pulled her dress down over her knees.

"Bertie Fobham will be along in a minute," she said.

"If he got out of the water butt," I said. "He's probably followed the van."

"Yes, the van. What's going on between you and Noisy?" she said.

"Nothing," I said.

66

She studied me. Then she gave that small shake to her head which either meant she was changing her mind about something or telling a whopper. She sat up straight.

"All right," she said. "Have it your own way. I'll tell you something. They're *his* bloody birds. Not mine. I kept them. I knew he'd come for them. I wanted him to, that's why I kept them. Now he's got them, he can keep them. That's funny—I don't want to see him any more. He's sweet, I was mad about him and I was damn pretty when I married him—but from a woman's point of view, he's no good. He wants a mother. Someone to pet him," she said slyly, "and cash his cheques."

"He told me he was going to get the birds. I thought it was one of his jokes," I said. I told her the story.

"Honour bright?" she said, like a schoolgirl. Then she added, "Typical Noisy to come and peep through the window. I expect he's fallen for your Claudia."

She glanced shrewdly to see how I would take that.

"All right," she said. "Another failure. Wash it out. That's the rotten attractive thing about him—he likes risk."

It was no good sitting there. Lord Fobham was obviously not coming to look for us. There were never any cars on that road at this time of night. It was unlikely there would even be a night lorry. It was four miles to Tolton, the nearest garage. I moved to get out.

"Where are you going?" she said, pulling my arm.

"I'm going to walk to Tolton to get some petrol," I said.

"I'm not going to stay here alone to be raped by some gamekeeper and I'm not going to walk," she said, "not in these shoes." I sat back.

"So that's that," I said. "What are we going to do?"

"That's that," she said. "What are you worrying about?"

"Claudia," I said. "Who's going to take her home?" She considered this.

"The Major," she said. "I'm sure he clocks her in and out, doesn't he?"

"Yes, he does."

Mrs. Brackett moved towards me.

"Poor Mr. Fraser," she said putting her arm in mine and resting her head on my shoulder. "Always in car trouble."

Yes, I thought, the Major will fetch her. And with that, my conscience was set free. I moved Mrs. Brackett's arm away and she sat up with annoyance for a second, then I put my arm round her and she put her head on my shoulder again.

"Mr. Fraser," she said. "You're an old hand, aren't you? I bet you'll kiss me next."

I did kiss her.

"Well that took a long time," she said. "About a year by my reckoning. All right, don't speak." She suddenly laughed.

"Do you know, when Bertie Fobham offered me fifty pounds for those birds I nearly closed on it. We could have loaded them up ourselves."

I kissed her again. She drew away from me and said:

"I suppose you know what you're doing?"

"No, I don't," I said and I was speaking the truth. I tried to pull her to me, but adroitly she opened the door of the car and stepped out.

"Let us walk up and down," she said, "and listen to the owls." And so we walked up and down a hundred times, I should think, asking me questions about myself, the shop and about Mother; she talked about the first time I went up to Heading to ask her to pay her bill.

"Gosh!" she said.

"You're lucky," she went on. "You've got your head screwed on."

We must have walked up and down until two in the morning and then there were lights on the road. A lorry came along after all. We siphoned some petrol and then drove back.

"You drive," she said and I did, with my arm round her waist. I could feel the heat of her face through my jacket. There was no one at Heading, of course, when we got there. At a quarter to three Claudia rang up while Mrs. Brackett and I were having a drink. I explained to Claudia what had happened. She said simply:

"Oh! Why aren't you at home?"

And rang off.

I don't know what time I got home. Now and then through the breaking mackerel sky, the September moon dodged in and out as I drove back. No longer the big yellow moon of the night when I got myself engaged to Claudia, but white, half gone and tipped up. It seemed as it went in and out of the clouds to be turning towards me and turning away, like Mrs. Brackett's busy, chattering head when the chase was on. The next morning Claudia broke off our engagement. Mrs. Dingle and the Major sent the announcement to *The Times*.

*   *   *

Mother didn't say anything until the afternoon. She shut herself up in the office and went through the bills.

"Staying out all night round the lanes with a married woman ten years older than yourself," Mother said. "I don't blame the girl."

The word "lanes" meant only one thing to Mother.

"Two pounds three—what is this?" said Mother, reading from a bill. "I'm glad you're out of it. Now we'll get some work done."

"I'd still be in it," I said, "if you hadn't let Noisy wheedle the van out of you."

"He brought it back. It's in the garage, you can see it. He thanked me. I don't often get thanks."

She looked wistfully at another bill and then at me.

"I don't know what he is up to and I wouldn't believe him if he told me. I knew he'd break his promise and not go back to her." She sighed with pleasure. "A woman's a fool who believes a word that comes out of Noisy."

Then Mother took off her glasses and began a tirade.

"And another thing. I may be an old woman—but don't think I'm blind. Don't think I don't know what brought Mrs. Brackett down here, paying her bill, as large as life, asking you up there and all that la-di-da soft soap about how pleased I must be and that this Claudia was the most wonderful girl in the world. I said to her 'Well, Mrs. Brackett, it will work itself out one way or the other, won't it? I could put my oar in, but I won't. It never lasts with him and I'm not breaking my heart.' "

Mother paused. A memory distracted her.

"The second time she came, she bought three dozen meringues," she said. "Did she give you any last night? Well, they keep."

"But," said Mother getting up from Father's old desk and flushing up with temper. "If you think I talked Mrs. Brackett into breaking it up, you're a very wicked boy . . ."

"I didn't say anything of the sort," I said.

"Think, I said, not say," said Mother.

And after that, I did begin to think and the more I thought the more I remembered what Father used to say about Mother's conscience.

Mother put her hand on the desk.

"Oh, you've upset me, with all this love," she said. She had gone pale. She had frightened herself.

"And now I suppose it will be Mrs. Brackett down here day and night, forty-five if she's a day, buying meringues and congress tarts until she's sick and you'll be hiding, all innocent, in the bakehouse, leaving it to your Mother. I wouldn't be that woman's dressmaker."

Mother went to the mirror over the mantelpiece and fiddled with her hair. "Age is what you feel," she said, getting ready for the battle.

NOISY IN THE DOGHOUSE

3

Noisy in the Doghouse

"SORRY to hear about you and Claudia, Bob", Noisy Brackett said, finishing a glass of beer and leaving me at the Crown one morning. "The Fairy Queen on the job again, I suppose? Take a tip from me. The next time you get engaged to a lovely thing like Claudia, steer clear of Fairy Queens. They turn funny when they see another girl get her man. Their little brains start working."

Noisy knew the whole story. Everyone in our town knew it. When I walked up the street, everyone from the dogs upward was silently giving me advice: "Fall for a divorced woman, ten years older than yourself [and some said twenty]—don't be a fool, boy!" I despised them all, but not Noisy. He had been married to her, I was in love with her; he and I were the only normal men in the town, and that was a thought I clung to. For the more I loved her the more I wanted to be saved from her, and Noisy was a living example of that salvation.

One good thing—the weather broke. Gales blew over the countryside and tore down the telephone wires. We were cut off from Heading for a day or two. Mother had a fright when the chimney caught fire at the back of our bakery; she thought the shop had gone. This, and the sign blowing off at the café, kept me outside and out of her sight. She had got as nervy as the weather. When I got in, I would find her sitting beside Father's photograph, which stood on a table by the window. She would get up and move about the room, trying the brown

leather chair of the three-piece first, but it disagreed with her in some way. She moved to the next chair and glared back at the other as if it had deceived her. But now her arms couldn't settle to this one either, and she lifted her elbow to see why. Then her knees got annoyed, and with a groan she got up and returned to the upright chair by the window and turned Father's photograph an inch or so to the light, as if she were trying to shake him into talking to her.

This happened night after night. While Mother was doing this, I had one eye on her and one on the newspaper, but my mind was four miles away, up at Heading with Mrs. Brackett, trying to catch sight of her face as it floated by, but all I could see was the drawing-room there and its three white-painted doors—the door she and I had come in by that night, the open door leading to the room where her farming papers were scattered over the floor, and a third door at the end of the room, which was closed. I never knew a door so closed. It watched us like a conscience. It seemed even to watch me now when I was at home. I could hear Mrs. Brackett saying, "What are you doing here at this time of night, Mr. Fraser?" But the only thing I could remember was the parting in her hair, for she had kept her head lowered when she was sitting beside me. After that, I would try without any luck to see again that small movement in the pupils of her blue eyes, a movement as tiny as the click of a camera shutter, when she looked up to say goodbye. I was going to say, "Where does that door lead to?" but the sight of her eyes taking a cool snapshot of what was going on inside me stopped me, and like a fool, I left.

I used to look at Mother over my paper. She would be staring at me, afraid of me and herself. We could not go on like this. So one evening when I came in from the Crown, I dived into it. I thought I would make her laugh. "Major Dingley says I ought to be horsewhipped," I said.

No answer from Mother.

"He said it to Lord Fobham over at the Crown. Noisy told me," I said.

Mother was still silent, but when Noisy's name came up she reached for her handbag and looked for the mirror.

"Lord Fobham said—" I went on.

"I don't want to know what Lord Fobham or any of those pots said," Mother said.

And she didn't. Mother thought it was wrong to know what people like that talked about, just as she mistrusted foreigners. They were "daft", and she was sorry for them.

"He said, Lord Fobham said," I went on, " 'Can't do that. Can't horsewhip a man any more. No horses. Nothing but cars. The roads weren't made for them.' "

"Where's the cleverness in that?" Mother said. "We know who needs the tanning. The telephone's working again. She's been on the line three times this morning. I told her you were out."

Mrs. Brackett, of course! She was after me!

"What did she order?" I said, playing it light.

"Order!" said Mother. "She was a good customer till you and her husband went stark staring mad."

We were silent again. I thought of something else; I had heard a rumour going round.

"Teddy Longfellow says Noisy's got an Argentine girl now—an air hostess," I said. "They say he's going to marry her." I couldn't have said anything worse if I'd tried. I thought Mother was going to hit the ceiling, burst, have a heart attack, or die. I'd never seen her face go so purple, then almost black. It nearly doubled its size. Her voice was always loud, but now she shouted, "I won't have you going over to the Red Lion like this." (I don't know why she always called the Crown the Red Lion.) "You know what drink did to your father. Teddy Longfellow was a German spy in the war. He signalled. Don't ask me who he signalled to, but he signalled. Everyone knows he signalled."

And Mother jumped up, went to the window, and pulled the blind down three inches, as if she, too, were signalling, but for the Army or someone to come and help her defend the country. If she had seen Noisy, or if she had seen Teddy Longfellow scratching his beard— he always picked at his beard at one corner of his mouth when he talked—she would have called out, "Help! I'm signalling. Didn't you see it? I'm signalling. Come in. You've upset me, both of you."

"Chinese air hostess!" she turned, raging on me. "There aren't any Chinese here. Don't be a fool."

"Argentine," I said.

"You're always contradicting what I say," she said. She sat down and became fretful. "He can't," she said. "He's a married man."

"He's divorced," I said.

"You keep telling me that. I'm not deaf," she said. "The rat—why did he let her?"

There was a long silence; she was frightened by what she had said. At last she became calm. She took out her handkerchief, in case she was going to need it.

"I didn't mean that—not rat," she said. She put her handkerchief back in her bag. Then she scowled. "Argentine meat," she said mournfully. "Your Father would never touch it."

And then Mr. Pickering, the solicitor, came over to see us.

"Good evening, Mrs. Fraser," said Mr. Pickering. "The wind's still bad, but you've got the bloom of spring on you."

His nose, Mother said to me afterwards, had the bloom on it, too. We were waiting for him; in fact, that is why Mother had on her dark-blue dress and had her handbag beside her. A lucky thing had happened, and if it hadn't I think I might have gone mad with my mind fixed on Mrs. Brackett. The Mill House at Galeford Priors had come up for sale privately, and Mother and I jumped at the chance of it—Mother because she liked a bit of property, and I because I knew it was cheap and because, as Father used to say, "Nothing clears the mind like buying property. It sobers you up."

But buying the Mill House gave us only a small respite. Since the night Claudia had broken our engagement I had neither seen nor spoken to Mrs. Brackett. I did everything to stop myself. I'd go out in the car and make it go the other way. I'd walk up to the telephone and all round it, but I never lifted the receiver. I spent my time thinking of new things to do. I mended the sign on the café. I even whitewashed one wall of the garage, and though I thought I had painted her out with every brushstroke, she came up through the paint. But that evening, after Mr. Pickering left, I had almost come to the end of everything that could prevent me trying to see her. I tried the usual little actions. I went round to the bakehouse to talk to the men. I came back and washed and shaved. I changed out of my working clothes. I put on my grey suit, but nothing happened, so I changed out of it into my brown. I came downstairs. There was only one thing left for me. I said to

Mother, "Let's go into Wetherington to the pictures."

"Get me my coat," Mother said, "I'm going out. Don't gape at me. I suppose your mother can go out, too?"

Mother's temper was the worst side of her; it is the same with me.

"Go on, get out!" she cried. "Go and chase your fancy woman. I'm not stopping you. I want to telephone."

Every family has its terrible sentences. Mother did not often answer the telephone, except in the shop, and when I was a child, if Mother announced she wanted to "use the telephone" she meant that everyone must get out of the house. Father used to say she would like the street cleared, too.

I left her, but you see the situation I was in; there was nothing to stop me going up to see Mrs. Brackett. Nothing at all. I got out my car, but I was too startled to know where to drive, and, in fact, I just drove to the end of the town, then round it, and came back again to the cross-roads near our house to see if the lights were on. I drove out of the town again and then did the same journey once more, because I couldn't remember *which* lights were on. The second time they were all out.

All idea of going up to Mrs. Brackett's went. Mother's mysteriousness saved me. I found myself going south to Wetherington at last and I was glad. Mrs. Brackett's house was in exactly the opposite direction, and every mile I put between her and myself made me gladder. It was one of those clear black evenings when the sky has been cleaned up by the wind and the stars have been brushed as bright as buttons, and if you had asked me after half an hour where I was going, I would have said I didn't know, I was just letting the car take me where it wanted.

81

Then I woke up. I had seen a signpost and I knew suddenly where I had been going all the time, where I had been thinking of going for a week or more without knowing it. I was going to see Noisy. I was only two miles from his new house. I drove faster. All the feelings that had weighed me down for a couple of weeks fell off. Good old Noisy! Once I saw him I would be all right. If there was one person who could save me from Mrs. Brackett, it was her ex-husband.

*   *   *

There is a stony lane up to Noisy's cottage. I had never been there in his time, but I knew where it was. I had once sheltered there with Claudia in a storm when it was a ruin. I remember she had been afraid there would be bats when we went upstairs, but there weren't. This cottage was on Teddy Longfellow's estate and stood under a row of beeches that sighed all the time—very rare trees in our part of the country. The land around it used to be grazing land, but Teddy had changed all that. Noisy had been living there for the best part of a year, after the divorce, rebuilding the place on his own. He was good with his hands and very patient.

I drove up to the cottage. It lay back behind new high wooden palings with a wide gate. The first thing I saw gave me a start; it was Brewster's cab and Teddy Longfellow's car beyond it. Beery Brewster was the taxi-driver in our town. I got out and went to open the gate, but I couldn't open it. I switched on my torch. I saw through a crack that there was a sort of lever and a bolt on it, and, on the gatepost, a bell. A bell in the country! And then I saw there was a wire running from the other side of the gate to an upper window of the cottage. I pressed the bell. A light came on over the front door and then another in the bedroom above, and the bedroom window opened and a grey-haired old woman with a shawl over her put her head out.

"Who is it?" she screeched in a nasal voice.

"Bob Fraser!" I called out. I put the light of my torch on her face. It gave a sudden twitch to the left eye that I would have recognized anywhere.

"Put that light out!" Noisy called out in his wartime voice. The wire squeaked, the gate opened. I went in, and Noisy was at the door with a wig in his hand and the shawl on his shoulders.

"Come in. We've quite a party in here. Welcome to the doghouse. Why didn't *you* bring your mother? Old Brewster's dead drunk in the kitchen. She had a terrible drive."

Sitting by the fire in Noisy's little sitting-room, comfortable and happy, was Mother, with a glass of whiskey in her hand.

"Oh, put that silly wig away," Mother said, laughing at him. "You frightened me out of my life. I hate those things. No!" screamed Mother. For Noisy had put the wig on again.

"It keeps away the undesirables," Noisy said to me, underlining the word, giving a twitch to his face. "Request permission to land. Permission refused." He took the wig off and admired it. "The old lady is like a mother to me. I'll get you a drink."

I sat down next to Mother, and she muttered, "What are you following me about for? Who looks a fool now?" And she nodded at the wig. "Argentine hostess —*you'd* believe anything."

And Mother laughed, united with herself and comfortable for the first time for weeks. "Teddy Longfellow's here," she whispered to me, anxious to make her call on Noisy at this hour respectable. And she straightened her dress. "What have you come here for? Haven't I got a life?"

Mother gave me a short, sharp rap on the knee to stop me replying, for Teddy Longfellow came in.

"Here, Teddy," said Noisy, handing him a drink.

"You haven't cut down those blasted f-fir trees yet, I see," said Teddy, fingering his beard at the end of his lower lip. His stammer, Noisy said, was worth ten thousand a year to him; it doubled his consonants and his income.

Teddy Longfellow scared everyone in our neighbourhood and enjoyed doing it. With his beard and the twist he gave to his hair and his eyebrows, he indeed looked like the devil. He used to alarm the parson during the war by praising Hitler, and annoy the hunting people by calling foxhounds "those ruddy useless dogs". Teddy liked causing trouble; it was he who had started this tale about Noisy's Argentine girl and—it turned out—had given him the wig. And, of course, he helped Noisy get his case of stuffed birds back from Heading, from under Mrs. Brackett's nose, and had pinched our van to do it. As he sat there he eyed Mother and me to see if he could see any more chances of annoying us.

"I said when are you going to c-c-cut down those firs?" Teddy said.

"No can do," said Noisy. "Useful for emergency landings in poor visibility. When I get them in line I know I'm bang on the runway."

"You won't get off the ground when the bomb drops anyway," said Teddy.

"You don't think there will really be a bomb, do you, Mr. Longfellow?" Mother said anxiously to Teddy.

"Bob," said Noisy. "Come out here. I'll show you the place. I can't bear to see that swine falling for the woman I love."

And Noisy gave me a peculiar look. I have often thought of it since. I got up and went out of the room with him.

"Now," said Noisy. "Here's the passage. All my own work. I did every bit myself. I put in those two doors. These stairs were rotten; I had to replace half the treads. Come up. Oak, my boy, solid oak. Yes, I did all the painting. Made a bathroom. The geyser was falling to bits. I got a nice lad down at the airport to fix it for me. See? Hot. Cold. I did all the plumbing."

He turned on the taps. All the pipes in the house jumped, whistled, and thundered.

"Beautiful sound, isn't it? Nothing like your own plumbing. Don't go away," he said. "Look at this. You sit in the bath, pull this ring—front gate closed, no one can get in. Pull this—open it. Front door, too. Wonderful what you can do if there are no women about. You see the idea? They can't get at you. Radio silence."

He led the way downstairs.

"Follow me," he said. "You haven't seen all. I've got something rather special here. You'll appreciate it."

He led the way down the passage to a locked door. It had a small shuttered hole in the middle of it. He unlocked the door. Inside was a tiny room, no larger than a keep pantry. It contained an armchair as wide as the room, a shelf with a gramophone on it, a wireless, a book or two, a few tins of food, and a lot of tools neatly arranged on the walls.

"What are these?" I said.

"Those? Wire clippers. Got them in the Service; you can cut through a half-inch bar with them. Very useful."

85

There were indeed several wires running through carefully made holes in the walls. He pulled one or two wires.

"Puts on red light outside. Warns them off . . . Shuts up garage . . . Turns on bath . . . Opens shutter on door, so you can see who's there. Press button, klaxon goes off in their face—no spies." Noisy stood back and made a statement. "You see the idea? Doghouse. Every house ought to have one. Make your own doghouse comfortable."

But I was looking at something else. There was hardly space for the two of us to stand in the little room, but against the wall was the life-size figure of a young girl in uniform, cut out of cardboard—an air hostess advertising the Argentine Air Lines, smiling at us. She was beckoning.

"Ah," said Noisy. "You've seen her! What a peach, Bob! What a dish! Never says a word, just stands there day and night, always a welcome."

Noisy stopped and looked at me, in a way half threatening, for he stuck out his thin chest. "Don't go near her," he said, "or I'll kill you."

And then slowly a dry grin came to one side of his mouth. "If you're ever in trouble—you know what I mean, the only trouble there is—here you are. Just pop-along to the doghouse. I mean it. I trust you. Come along. I mean if the Fairy Queen gets on your tail, starts throwing the television about or burning your clothes on the sitting-room fire or trying to get your medals into slot machines. I say just let the air out of her tyres and buzz off down here. It's all yours. I've packed in all that sort of thing now. There's my girl now." He pointed to the cardboard figure. "I've given her the key to my heart." He had hung that large rusty key on a nail stuck in the back of the model. "And, by the way, that reminds me! Testing, testing, testing, zero, one, two, three, four —she rang up to see if you were here an hour ago."

"Who?" I said.

"My ex-wife," said Noisy, giving me the pistol shot with his eye.

He stared at me as if waiting for me to fall. Then he laughed. "It's all right. I told her you weren't here. And, that's funny, you weren't! Be a good fellow, for God's sake, and ring her up or something. I don't want her blinding down here in the middle of the night looking for you. Go *now*," he said. "You know what women are. I had to put up the barricades when my other wife— the first one—dropped down here six months ago. She'd heard I was nesting. She brought two kids with her. I don't know where she got them. Now let's see what that swine Teddy is up to."

We went into the sitting-room just as Mother was saying, "If you could only tell the future, I mean, Mr. Longfellow, you would know what was going to happen."

She glared at me when I came into the room. She was on to her old subject, and Teddy was politely nodding.

"Bob's got to go off," said Noisy, but I sat down. I didn't leave at once, and when I did I took Mother with me. She was upset.

"I could wring that Noisy's neck," she said in the car. "I could limb him, playing a trick like that. Spreading all that daft stuff with a wig. No woman would go and live at a place like that. What were you doing outside?"

"Looking for the air hostess," I said.

"That's all pansy stuff. What's clever in it?"

So I said nothing, for now that she was with me she was fighting herself again.

Something must have happened to me at Noisy's—I don't know what—but the next evening I went up to Mrs. Brackett's. I didn't even ring her first. I just went.

It was always quiet up at Heading. Through the trees by the house you could see the stars, and the grey stone was lit by them. There was a smell of cows and wood smoke, and there was a touch of frost in the air. I passed the maid going home on her bicycle as I was going up. The curtains were not drawn, and I could see two lamps burning in the long sitting-room. The front door was open, and after I had rung the bell I walked in the wide hall where Noisy's case of birds had once stood—the marks of the stand were still on the carpet—and I called out, "Anyone at home?"

All the white doors in the hall were closed except one leading to the drawing-room. I listened. Then I heard talking; Mrs. Brackett was speaking on the telephone. I went farther in and I heard her say "There's someone here", but she still went on talking. More I couldn't catch until two or three words made me stop. She was saying the name of that horse again: "Tray [or something or other] Pays On." Exactly the words she had said two years or more ago, the second time I came up to ask her to pay our bill, and when she made all the trouble about it and I was afraid of her. I wasn't afraid of her now and I wasn't afraid of the house and all its things. The three or four big pictures in the room even looked smaller and the chairs rather shabby.

I heard her ring off and she came out fast from the room. When she saw me, the telephone look went dead on her face. She hesitated and then said, "Hullo! That was Kitty Fobham." Then she shook her head and said, "Actually, it wasn't."

Does that make two lies? I don't know: the moment

she boldly said them she lowered her head and put out a foot as if she were sketching something in a hurry on the carpet, and then took a few steps aside before she looked at me again. She had a real liar's walk. It was her body that told the lies—I mean the way she walked, how her hips moved and her arms. Her tongue, I must say, usually told the truth. If it didn't, her head gave that shake to warn you she was going to try something on. That was why people who spread stories about her really liked her. And when I say her body told lies, I mean they were the kind of lies any man likes to hear.

"They told me you telephoned," I said.

"Why didn't you ring me back?" she said.

"I've come instead," I said.

"You don't say! Well, sit down. I've been washing my hair," she said. She pointed to the deep, green settee where we had sat the night that had ended my engagement with Claudia. It was too low for me; I'm tall.

Mrs. Brackett looked plain. There was a line across her forehead, and her hair was darker because it was wet. It ended in rat-tails, just like the hair of a maid we used to have years ago. Mrs. Brackett went to the far side of the fireplace and held her hair down to dry it by the fire. We both spoke at once.

She said, in her cattle dealer's voice, "I wanted to see you. I expect you think it was my fault Claudia broke up with you. I'm sorry."

I said, "What is this 'Pays On'? 'Say Pays On'? 'Tray Pays On'? You said it on the telephone."

"Pays on?" she said, throwing her hair back and looking at me. "What d'you mean? On the blower—I said that?"

"I don't know," I said. "You said it once before, when I came up here years ago, as well, about the bill."

She smiled. "Still on about the bill," she said. "What's the matter? Haven't you paid your water rates? I don't know what you're talking about. 'Pays on'? Never heard of it." And she lowered her head to the fire. "I'll never get this dry," she said.

"That's it. Pays On," I said. "Is it a horse? Noisy said it was a horse."

She sat up and again threw her hair back from her broad low forehead when she heard Noisy's name.

"When I came up here," I went on. "Noisy said it sounded like one of those French horses."

"A French horse? I never heard . . ." She stopped. She opened her mouth and put her tongue in her cheek, like a child caught stealing. She got up and walked over to a side table where the drinks stood. I watched the way she walked. She was wearing one of her terrible dresses of blue stuff with little yellow and red daisies on it. It looked like someone else's. And a tomato-coloured cardigan. I remember her saying, the night when Claudia and I had dinner there, that it puts a woman "one up in the conver" if you give a man a shock at the sight of your clothes and it "makes the other women look sick".

"A horse." She laughed. "What will you have to drink?" she said, turning round. "Noisy told you that?"

"Yes."

"Well," she said. "I will tell you." And she spoke like someone spelling out to a child. "It's not a horse, it's a man. A Frenchman who lives in the country. It's French."

"Nothing for me," I said. "Why talk in French. Is it smart or something?"

"You're a suspicious character, Bob," she said. "You sound sore. What's the matter? Has flour gone up? Can't you sell your cream puffs?"

I kept my temper, because her voice had changed and was soft.

"Let's see," I said. "He's a man. And he's French. And he lives in the country. He wouldn't be a peasant, would he?"

"Good!" she said, laughing. "That's it—a French peasant. A real peasant."

I nodded. " 'Bloody peasant,' Noisy said," I said, giving a scratch behind my ear.

She gave me a long look, which died away, and she said outright, "All right, you win. I was talking about you."

"That's funny," I said. "Noisy thought it was a horse."

"Noisy has better manners than me. Can we drop it?"

"What?" I said. "Is it something insulting? I didn't know that. What's wrong with it? It's no worse than silly bitch, is it?"

I thought Mrs. Brackett was going to fly at me, but she didn't. She stuck her chin out. She said quietly, seriously, "I apologize."

"That's all right," I said. "It's best to begin with a row."

"Damn, damn, damn," she said. "I really do apologize. Honour bright." And then her eye gave that little flick. "Begin what?" she said.

I got up to walk over to the table to her.

"No," she said. "Stay where you are. If you don't want a drink, I do." I sat down again, but when she brought her drink, she came over to my side of the fireplace and sat on the stool there. We were silent for quite a time.

"I've bought the Mill House," I said.

"That's nice of you," she said. "You've changed the subject. How did you hear about it?"

She was sharp where there was a question of a deal. I told her about it. I said I thought of turning it into an hotel, and we argued about that a long time—how you'd never get a manager in a place like that.

"How much did you give for it?" she said.

I didn't answer, but—it just came into my head, and I didn't mean it—I said, "How would *you* like to manage it?"

She was as surprised as I was. "I don't like being mocked," she said. "Is that what you came up to say? Of course I wouldn't manage your hotel. Anyway, it's a crime to do anything like that with that place. D'you always go about sitting in cars with women and then ask them to manage hotels. Did you ask Claudia? Why are you so mad about money?"

Jealous! I pricked up my ears. The room seemed to smile at me. There was a picture on one of the walls of a lot of cardinals drinking wine, and the central one had his smiling face turned toward us. Even the white door at the end of the room might have opened; I wouldn't have been surprised.

"She was only a girl of nineteen," I said. "Since Father died, I am responsible."

"Pooh. You're only twenty-two yourself."

"Thirty," I said.

"How old d'you think I am?" she said, putting her head back and moving to the sofa. In a way, she looked her worst, but I wasn't looking at her face. I remember Noisy once saying he was twenty-three hundred years old and that she was twelve.

"Twelve," I said.

"I'm thirty-three," she said, giving the short shake to her head. "Actually, thirty-six. And don't copy Noisy."

Thirty-six, I was thinking—that will be something to tell Mother the next time she starts on me about Mrs. Brackett's age. When I looked at her again, she was very friendly.

"I'm selling this house, if you're in the buying mood," she said. "I can't afford it."

I shook my head. "Why don't you sell it to Teddy Longfellow?" I said. "I saw him at Noisy's last night. He's rich."

She started. "The liar!" she said, blushing. "Noisy said you weren't there."

"I wasn't when you rang," I said.

She smiled and leaned toward me. "Did you see this girl of his, the Argentine girl everyone is talking about?"

I was the biggest fool in the world, I felt so confident of her.

"Yes," I said carelessly, and I laughed.

"What is she like—young? I'm glad he's got a girl."

I was in it; I had to go on. "Yes, young," I said.

"Is she tall?" Mrs. Brackett moved nearer to me. "Tell me what she's like."

"Dark," I said. "Yes, tall."

"Taller than me? Pretty? What is she like? What did she say?" She started arranging her hair as she talked.

"Taller," I said. "A bit—kind of stiff. I've only seen her in uniform. She didn't say much. No, I don't think she said anything. Teddy Longfellow was there, and Mother. Something dead about her."

"Is she working? I mean is she air-hostessing still?"

I was beginning to enjoy this.

"I think they've grounded her."

"Why?" Mrs. Brackett said anxiously.

"I don't know," I said.

"You must have some reason," she said.

"She just looked grounded."

"How can anyone look grounded? She sounds like a dummy to me," said Mrs. Brackett, with an unnatural laugh. "Stiff as a board, in uniform. Doesn't she speak? Poor Noisy—serves him right. He likes a chat."

She put her hand on my arm and said excitedly, "I'll tell you what we'll do. Let's go and see them. I'll ring him up."

"No," I said, alarmed by what I'd said.

"Yes," she said, moving away, but I caught her arm and held her.

"My hair is wet," she said, shaking to get away, but I held her arm and presently she stopped pulling.

"Please," she said. "You're hurting me." I slackened my hold and she got up at once. She was a trickster.

"I'm going to see them," she said, looking at her watch and going toward the door.

"It's ten o'clock," I said. "They'll be in bed."

Mrs. Brackett stopped at the door. She went very white. With her hair plastered down and her mouth suddenly small and her eyes startled as if I had hit her, she looked ugly.

"That," she said, coming back a step to me, "was a dirty remark."

"Trays Pays On," I said.

She looked as if she would throw something, if there had been anything near. Then her eyes almost closed and she laughed and laughed and came and sat down near me. "You're not the same as when you first came up here. What has happened to you?" she said softly to me.

"Nor are you," I said, moving toward her.

She began pulling at the thread of the settee as she

94

had done before. I can't remember what we said, but we did get on to the subject of the door at the end of the room and where it led to. To the second staircase, she said. And one thing led to another.

* * *

The next morning, when I had seen to the vans, I rang her. I was mad to hear her voice. There was no reply. Several times I rang, and there was no answer. Mother came into the room behind the shop to look at me, and everytime the phone rang, she and I moved to it. At last I had to go to Wetherington in the afternoon —it was early closing with us, and Mother wanted to come with me and go shopping. There was something secretive about Mother, because she wouldn't, as she usually did, tell me where to pick her up in the town. Usually, I found her outside the biggest draper's, but today she wouldn't say for a long time, and then she said, "In the station yard." This puzzled me. She had what we used to call her broody look, like a hen sitting heavily, and occasionally she'd break out into the first line of a song, but stop because she could never remember the others. In the end, I met her at the station, looking comfortable and sly, as though she had eaten something good, and when we drove away, she was soft-tempered and dreamy. She had got her week of anger off her mind. We had been driving for twenty minutes when she said, "They don't tell you anything. It's daft. Your Uncle Dan in Canada has been dead for years."

She had been to a fortune-teller.

"Well, who else could it be?" she said.

We got back to the shop, and I drove into the yard at the side and straight for the garage, which I had left

95

open. It was dark now, and I had put the headlights full on. Just as the car was going into the garage, Mother clutched my arm and cried out "Stop, Bob! There's a woman there!"

She was right. There, standing against the white-washed wall, stood a tall young girl, smiling. For a moment I thought it was Molly Gibson; she was dark. Then I looked again. It was not a girl—not a living girl. It was Noisy's cardboard girl from the Argentine Air Lines.

"Oh, it gave me a turn, I thought you'd kill her," Mother said. "What is it? Who put it there?"

We got out. Mother looked at me suspiciously. It was what the fortune-teller had said, she told me: there'd be a visitor from overseas.

I examined the figure. "It's Noisy's," I said. "It's got the key to his heart hanging on the back."

Mother came and looked. Her face darkened. "You've upset Noisy. You don't listen to me. You've upset him. I could see it the other night." And Mother marched out of the yard, down the street to our house.

I knew Noisy was always playing the fool, but there was always something behind his jokes. And then—it was natural—I felt a bit uneasy about Noisy ever since I had fallen in love with Mrs. Brackett. He was friendly, but he had changed. I had once or twice caught him giving me a strange look, his face not twitching, but still as stone; his eyes very sharp, sarcastic.

I went to the bakehouse, but the men didn't know anything about the dummy. I went along to the café and asked the two girls there. Had Noisy been in, I asked the first girl.

"No," she said.

"Are you sure?" I asked.

The other girl came out of the kitchen.

"Has Noisy been in today? Any time?"

"No," said the girls.

I told them there was a poster in the garage.

"Oh," said the eager girl from the kitchen. "That was Mrs. Brackett. She left it this afternoon." And she gave me a knowing smile; I did not like it.

"Did she leave a message?" I said, not letting on. "You're sure it was Mrs. Brackett?"

"Yes," they said. And there was no message.

They were grinning behind my back when I left. I saw them in the mirror. You can imagine what was going on in my head. I didn't mind the joke, but Mrs. Brackett and Noisy in it together!

I went back to our house.

"Mrs. Brackett brought it," I said to Mother.

Mother ignored this. Her temper was rising. "Trying to make a laughing-stock of your mother!" she said. "Telling me he had an Argentine girl up there! Do you think anyone in his senses would believe a twopenny tale like that?"

"I didn't make it up," I said.

"I'm sure you didn't," she said. "You haven't the brains. All this love has made you stupid. Going about with your mouth wide open, you'd swallow anything, and the business goes to ruin. Two customers complained the bread was burned yesterday—the whole lot. The whole town's laughing at you. Noisy's taken your measurements, my boy. Running after another man's wife! They've made fools of you. And I am glad. It will teach you a lesson. And don't ask me to be sorry. I told you this divorcing was all my eye. Oh, I wish your father was alive!"

"Why would they put it there?" I said. "Anyway, it was Mrs. Brackett."

I was going to say more; I was in a temper, too. I went round to the shop again and I sat at the desk staring at the telephone, and then I rang Mrs. Brackett.

"I have been trying to ring you," I said.

"That is a change," she said. "Is anything the matter?"

Her voice sounded cold.

I laughed. It was so lovely to hear her. "Well," I said. And I laughed again.

"What is the joke?" she said.

I was still laughing as I began. "I—"

"Are you ringing me up about that dummy?" she said sharply. "You are? You found it? Bad luck for you. Listen. I don't like being mocked. I had ten years of that kind of thing with Noisy."

God, I thought. Mother storming at me at home, and Mrs. Brackett shouting from up on the hill.

"I don't want any more stableboy jokes." Mrs. Brackett had a temper. We all had tempers, I suppose— Mother, me, Mrs. Brackett, and all of us.

She slammed down the telephone.

I would have let her temper go and waited for her to cool off and to come running down. What stopped me was not my own temper, but what was clearer every moment I thought of it: that she and Noisy had got together again, for how else could she have got hold of the dummy?

*   *   *

I ran into the yard, and that damn silly thing was still smiling away at me as I got into the car. I drove up to Heading. I was mad. The servant was coming down on her bicycle, just as I had seen her two days before. This time I could have gladly knocked her over.

But Mrs. Brackett was not at Heading. She had gone out. I came slowly back to the shop. I did not know what to do. Several times my hand went to the telephone. I was tempted to ring Noisy to tell him what I thought of him, but I couldn't. I went over to the Crown.

And there I heard something that changed my mind. Teddy Longfellow was in the bar talking to the landlord, who was polishing glasses and lifting each one to his eye to see if it was clean as he listened.

"They cut fifty pounds' worth of wire", Teddy was saying.

"He told me that on the phone," said the landlord.

"Hullo, Bob," said Teddy. "Did you hear this?"

"What was that? Have they cut your wire?" I said to Teddy. He often had trouble with hooligans who let his cattle out.

"Up at Mr. Brackett's," said the landlord.

"Noisy's had burglars," said Teddy.

I looked at the landlord, for I never believed any tale that Teddy came along with, but the landlord put a glass down and said: "This afternoon. When he was out."

"Well they wouldn't do it when he was in!" said Teddy scornfully.

Yes. Out (I thought). With Mrs. Brackett, delivering that poster to me, but Teddy's next words put another light on it.

"I told Noisy just now it sounds like the job of a sex maniac to me," said Teddy to the landlord, "cutting all that wire, smashing a kitchen window—all to get at a woman! I told Noisy months ago it was a mistake to keep a foreign woman up there."

"What woman?" said the landlord.

"Bob knows her, don't you, Bob?" said Teddy.

That was enough for me. Noisy had not been with

Mrs. Brackett; in fact it was clear from the far-away tone of Teddy's voice that he was going to spread the rumour that *I* was with her. He was picking away at his beard fast, delighted with himself. It was clear he had had a peep into my garage.

What puzzles me now is why I didn't let it go at that. I suppose I was so relieved to see that Noisy and Mrs. Brackett were not in this together that I didn't stop to ask myself "Whose side are you on?" but went straight off eagerly to ring up Noisy. If only I hadn't rung him!

"This is going to cost you a pretty penny, Bob," Noisy said before I could get a word in. "A hundred feet of wire chopped up to bits, two locks gone, kitchen window smashed, geyser not working—add the men's time at union rates . . ."

"I don't know what you're talking about."

"And then," Noisy went on. "There's the emotional side. No one thinks of that nowadays. That's what I can't get over. Bob, you rotten free-lance, breaking up a happy home. Think of all those poor children crying, 'Where's Mummy? When's she coming back from the Argentine?' Tragedy of easy divorce, divided homes, one more little delinquent attacking women in parks, Father's sad evidence—"

"Listen, Noisy—"

"Bob, you bloody daylight burglar. Over."

"I've got her," I said. "She put her in our garage."

"Who did?"

"Your wife."

"My ex-wife, if you please," said Noisy.

"We found her when we got back from Wetherington this afternoon."

"Who's we?" said Noisy.

"Mother and I," I said.

101

"Mother in it, too," said Noisy. "My God! Radio silence, old boy. I'll be over in five minutes."

He came with his usual roar. "Let me see her," he said, and we went into the garage. He sniffed the air. "It's damp in here. Bad for the poor girl's chest." He looked at her proudly. "Isn't she a peach? Now, my sweetie," he said to her, "you stay where you are, do as you are told. It will be all right. We're going to lock you in, so you don't get up to tricks." And he closed the garage door.

"Aren't you going to take her back?" I said as he locked the door himself.

"Bob," he said very seriously, "when Teddy Longfellow and I broke into Heading that time and got my case of birds back, they were my birds, weren't they? We didn't steal anything, did we? We didn't touch a thing that wasn't our own—right? We didn't do any damage, did we? We didn't break a kitchen window and leave filthy footmarks on the floor, did we? One of the cleanest jobs you ever saw, I bet, wasn't it? And we didn't lift anything lying about, like a pair of service wire clippers, for example?" He was scowling. "Oh, yes," he said, "we're going to get them back. Jump in. I know her hideouts. We'll buzz up to Heading to see if the clippers are there, but if they're not they'll be in her car. And remember, Bob, for future reference"—he gave that twitch to his eye as he turned his head to me— "when the Fairy Queen takes off she's never got more than a gallon of gas in the tank. That cuts the target area down to eleven miles. She can't be at the Fobhams', for instance."

We were off. The roar of Noisy's car was unmistakable in our town, and of course it brought Mother to the door.

We tried Heading first—"the ancestral home", Noisy said—and drew nothing, then to the Duck outside Tolton, the Lamb at Forth Hill, then the Aylesbury Arms, the Green Man, and the Sailor's Return.

"Bob," said Noisy, getting whiter in the face after every pub, "the Fairy Queen is not one of those who, in the normal free-for-all, can dish it out but can't take it. Something must have got her on the raw."

I told him the story—well, three-quarters of it.

"Tall, dark girl, you said. Didn't talk much, you said? Very nice," he said, grinning. "Anything else?"

"I said I thought she was grounded," I said.

Noisy laughed loudly. "Wrong there, Bob," he said. "She's in uniform."

He became thoughtful. "Of course, I can see she was getting her own back on me, but why dump that lovely creature at *your* place? That's what foxes me."

We drove on, missing the Harrow at Denton Bridge, because the man there watered the gin. "There's only one more chance," Noisy said, driving now on the wrong side of the road. "Play the game or get out of the bed!" he shouted at a passing car.

We seemed to lose our way in by-lanes. Suddenly he pulled up at a pub called the Fox and stopped in the yard. We did not get out.

"The only thing I can think of, Bob, is you were making a pass at her. Yes, that's what it must have been," Noisy said as we sat there. "Never make a joke when you're making a pass at a woman. They don't like it. You're right down the drain if you do. And let me tell you, I don't care a damn if you *are* down the drain. But I want my wire clippers back. They've been with me in France, in Egypt, in India, and I've never seen the man who'd dare lay a finger on them."

We looked round the yard.

"What did I tell you?" said Noisy suddenly. "See that? She's here.

He pointed to Mrs. Brackett's car. We sat gazing at it.

"Keep your eyes skinned, Bob," said Noisy at last. He got out and went over to her car, opened the door, and looked around inside. He came back with the heavy pair of service wire clippers in his hand.

"Mission accomplished," he said. "Let's get drunker."

We considered the peaceful white walls of the inn, the bare trees, the lights shining behind the curtained windows.

"It brings back memories," said Noisy. "Many's the time we've finished up here, the Fairy Queen and I, after a row. Funny to think she's in there now, all on her own, knocking them back. Mind if I come in, too, for old time's sake?"

For I had begun to move for the door.

There was a loud noise coming from the bar, where the locals were, but we went into the small one. Sitting alone in a chair by the bar was Mrs. Brackett.

"Scotland Yard," said Noisy thickly, turning back the lapel of his coat.

Mrs. Brackett put her drink down and, looking at Noisy, she blushed. "I see you've brought the Sergeant," she said, glancing coldly at me.

"We didn't know whether this was going to be a strong-arm job, did we, Bob?" said Noisy. "It's all right, We're both drunk."

"Mr. Fraser's quite free with his arms, too," said Mrs. Brackett primly. "Why doesn't he sit down? Is he going?" For Noisy had sat down beside her.

"I'm mad about her, aren't you, Bob?" said Noisy. "A real bit of old Newgate, isn't she? No, Bob's not going."

"Well, why doesn't he join in the conversation?" said Mrs. Brackett. "Has flour gone up again? Or is he worried about his new girl?"

"Oh," cried Noisy, "has Bob got a new girl? He didn't tell me that. Bob, what's this, you rotten seducer? You never told me."

"A foreign girl—Argentine, I believe," said Mrs. Brackett. "Very dark, very tall. They'll make a handsome pair. She used to be an air hostess, isn't that so, Mr. Fraser? Grounded . . ."

"Much better grounded," said Noisy. "You know where they are."

"A bit stiff in her uniform," said Mrs. Brackett.

"That will wear off when they get married," said Noisy.

I laughed, but Noisy didn't and neither did Mrs. Brackett when she looked at me.

"With a fine fellow like Bob, of course it will," said Noisy. "Good-looking, too."

"Yes," said Mrs. Brackett. "And doing well. He's just bought the Mill House. He asked me to manage it. It's going to be an hotel."

"Go on!" said Noisy. "What? Eight ten a week and all found?"

"You won't know him in ten years' time. He'll have bought the town," said Mrs. Brackett.

"Well, all I can say," said Noisy, "I hope he's found the right woman."

"She sounds absolutely cut out for him," said Mrs. Brackett. "Has she got any money, Mr. Fraser?"

"*Mr.* Fraser, *Mr.* Fraser!" said Noisy in a shocked

way. "You don't seem to know each other too well. Come and sit over here, Bob, and get acquainted. This is Mrs. Brackett. Will you excuse me a minute?"

And Noisy went out.

"I love you," I said to Mrs. Brackett. "Let us go. Now."

Mrs. Brackett's face softened.

"I've been in love with you since I first saw you," I said.

"I was mad about *you*, actually," said Mrs. Brackett. "But"—giving a shake to her head—"I don't like technique."

"It was just a joke."

"Really?" said Mrs. Brackett. "Well, I haven't got a sense of humour. Ask Noisy."

"But last night you loved me," I said.

"Hold it a minute," she said. "I'll tell you."

She got up and went to the street door. "Noisy's a long time," she said. "Has he gone? I didn't hear him."

Then Noisy came in and met her there.

"I thought you'd gone," said Mrs. Brackett.

"No, my sweet, just taking the air," said Noisy, taking her arm. "Nice to be missed."

Mrs. Brackett hesitated.

"I'm going home," she said and suddenly pushed violently past him out of the pub.

We stared at the closed door. The closed door in the sitting-room at Heading came into my mind. I don't know what was in Noisy's, but we both went after her. At once we heard a shout from her across the yard.

"Bloody funny!" she shouted and came marching in a fury across the yard, opened the door of Noisy's car, and got in and slammed it. Noisy sauntered up to her.

"You damn well drive me!" she shouted at him.

Noisy turned to me, shrugged, and beckoned, but I was staring at her car. Someone had let the air out of the two back tyres. Suddenly, I heard Noisy's car roar. He had taken off.

*   *   *

Mrs. Brackett's car stood in our garage at home for three weeks. It took me twenty minutes to pump its tyres, and where she and Noisy went that night I do not know. I went after them. They weren't at Heading. They weren't at his cottage. Nor in the days, even the weeks that followed. The Post Office said they had gone abroad. The damp got into the hostess of the Argentine Air Lines. She peeled and she buckled and fell over. I told one of the men to pitch her in the dustbin. He brought the key hanging on the back to me, and I told him to throw that away, too. On second thoughts, I broke up the dummy girl myself.

Mother said nothing, but once or twice she goes on about the future—the usual thing. "If you knew what was going to be you'd act differently," she says. "People ought to tell you, then you'd know," she says. And then she gets on to Teddy Longfellow saying there isn't any future, and I tell her I agree with him. A few weeks ago, Heading came up for sale. Mother says the class of trade is changing in our town.

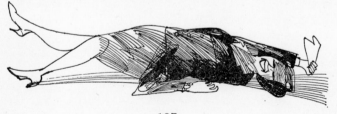

Printed in Great Britain by
W. & J. Mackay & Co Ltd

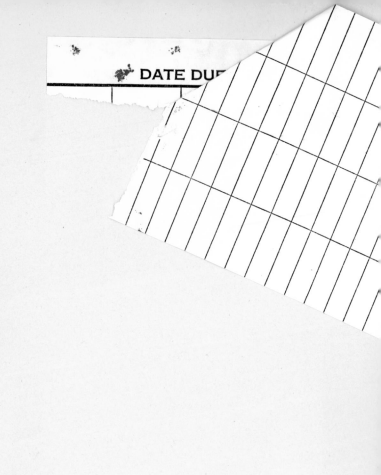

DATE DUE